Back of Forever: Vampire Mine

Elaine Waldron

A Symes-Mobberley House Publication

Table of Contents:

Prologue:

Count Gavril Conta was a handsome man; stood tall, a good six-foot-three, a wealth of dark hair and sideburns with a touch of gray; stately and regal in appearance, in spite of his hidden dark side few men witnessed, and the ones who had, soon wished they hadn't.

He lingered for some time, enjoying the light of the full moon reflecting down on the old castle ruins, the former home of his second cousin, Count Dracula. It wasn't Bran Castle, as so many mistook for Dracula's home, but Poenari Castle on the Arges River. He had since built a replica, the best he could from what he could remember of the old one, and now was his home when in Romania.

He seldom visited the ruins of the original, for it brought back many memories, powerful memories – blood, death, impaled corpses – when his cousin had ruled with terror and horror. Gavril had been thirty-eight when his cousin had finally met his demise. He smiled at the irony. Dracula had turned him shortly before he met his own death at Gavril's hands. Thirty-eight, Gavril would be forever. In actual years, he was fast approaching six hundred.

He heard Maxmillian, his faithful chauffeur of German descent and longtime confidant, calling from below. "Time to leave, sir. You'll miss your boat to America! Your coffin will travel without you."

"I'm coming, Max," he replied and took one last glance around at the broken walls and overgrowth, sniffed in the damp air, and headed down the path to the bottom of the hill where Maxmillian patiently waited, holding the limousine door open. He slid in and Maxmillian took his place behind the steering wheel, turned the car around and headed for the main road.

"I will miss you, sir," Maxmillian said, looking at him in the rearview mirror.

"And I, you. I am not sure how long I will be away… Could be a mere few months. A few years. Perhaps much longer. However, I will keep in touch. You know, I will come back occasionally, even if I decide to live there semi-permanently. I just need to see some new sights…" He smiled wickedly. "Taste some new blood."

Maxmillian reflected his smile. "Yes, sir."

"I haven't been to the states in almost a hundred years. I want to see just how much it has changed. Especially Seattle."

"Ah…yes! Seattle," he said reflectively. "I was there about ten years ago."

"This I did not know."

"I do not believe I ever told you. You had taken a vacation to Australia at the time. Had said I could take one too, if I desired. I went to visit Jorj, an old childhood friend, whose folks had moved there when he was fifteen… Seattle," he said again, "the city one might consider as an international gateway to the United States and other parts of the world, being in the North-West section of the country, with its ports, Puget Sound, and what have you…I understand perfectly, sir. I will keep a faithful eye on everything, as you know."

"I have no doubts that you will." Gavril laid his head back then and closed his eyes. Sleep wasn't something he needed, but sometimes he would doze off when he wanted time to pass more quickly.

Chapter One:

Mona Sims stood on the deck of the ferry as it headed from Port Orchard, Washington, where several hours prior she'd visited her mother before meeting up with Darren, her ex-fiancé, and was now headed back into Seattle, watching the frothing trail in the boat's wake in the hazy moonlight. Though chilled to the bone from the freezing mist and cutting wind, she didn't care. It was the numbness inside that controlled her, not the freezing cold on the outside. Darren, the man she had believed to be the love of her life, until just a couple of hours prior, had dumped her like yesterday's garbage.

He had said they needed to talk, and she was somewhat confused by the lack of luster in his voice when she met up with him at a coffee shop not far from the ferry dock, for rejection was not what she had anticipated. It also hit her as strange that he had come to Port Orchard to do so, when he could have spoken with her in Seattle. Was it because he was ashamed? Didn't want any of his friends and acquaintances to know what an actual jerk he really was? Probably, she surmised, now that she thought about it.

They had been dating for nearly six months and living together for five. What she had hoped for and expected was a proposal of marriage – not a breakup.

Shocked didn't even come close to what she felt. It was more like dead. That was it. She felt dead inside, as though her heart had stopped beating and she could no longer breathe. Only that wasn't the case. She was very much alive and definitely breathing. As she stood there watching the churning foam disappear into the murkiness of the dark water, vaguely aware of the shoreline lights of Seattle in the distance, she considered ending her pain by simply jumping overboard. As fate would have it, her attention was stolen by men shouting, and bright searchlights cutting through the night, as several of the crew members scrambled about the deck behind her. She turned to watch, wondering what all the urgency was about. Someone yelled, "Man overboard!" The ferry jolted and quickly slowed down, hissing loudly and then coming to a full stop.

Two shafts of lights beamed across the water behind, crossing one another as they were angled this way and that as the crew searched for the man. "There!" Someone shouted. "I see him there!"

Swirling back around, she saw a body floating in the water, a man in a white shirt and dark trousers, face down.

Suddenly a tall man dressed in a long, dark trench coat, collar raised and shrouding his face, stepped up not too far from her right to the railing and glanced at her. It was only for a moment, but she was immediately drawn into the shimmering black pools that were his eyes. He said nothing and turned his stare back to the water.

A small motorboat was thrown out over the side and a couple of crewmen lowered themselves down on ropes, climbed in and took off towards their man.

Watching and wondering if the man below was dead or alive, she forgot about Darren. One of the men yelled that they had him and the lifeboat headed back for the ferry. She heard what sounded as a low, sardonic chuckle and snapped her head around to meet those black eyes again – and gasped, for he now stood next to her. She had not even realized he had moved.

A thin smile came to his closed lips, which she recognized as perfectly shaped. Her gaze trailed up his aquiline nose. The stranger, though probably in his late thirties, was very handsome; dark hair with just a touch of silver on his short sideburns added to his regal air. So handsome, in fact, that really seeing him clearly for the first time took her breath away. He looked like a foreigner. She considered that he might be of Serbian descent because of his dark complexion.

"It seems they have their man," was all he said in a silky voice of resonating timbre, laced with an accent, and then, turning swiftly, he strode away.

Instantly fascinated and somewhat dumfounded by his mere presence, she couldn't help it, followed him with her eyes as he disappeared into the enclosed passenger section. She wondered where he had come from and where he had gone. He did not look like anyone she would expect to meet, not even in a place as Seattle, where people from all over the world and all walks of life moved in and out daily on their worldly travels.

Her attention returned to the lifeboat as it pulled up alongside the ferry, and other crew members went to assist in getting the man up first, and then laying him down to perform CPR, while others hoisted the lifeboat back onto the ferry. It was growing crowded where she stood, so she decided it best that she go inside too. The lights of Seattle were distinct now. They would be docking any minute. Pike Place Market was just to the right as one exited the ferry and then, a little further down, the drugstore where her apartment was, overhead.

She halfway expected to see the dark stranger when she went inside, but to her surprise, he wasn't anywhere in sight. Perhaps he had gone to the bathroom, which was up a small flight of stairs in the center of the cabin. Hoping to get a glimpse of the stranger again, she waited, out of curiosity, after they pulled into dock, where an ambulance and police cars awaited the ferry, but it was to no avail. The handsome stranger was nowhere to be seen.

After the body was taken off the ferry, the passengers were allowed to leave. She waited until all the cars were off, and there was only one other foot-passenger left to exit the ferry besides her, an elderly man with a backpack on his back, tapping along the exit ramp with a cane. She had no choice but to get off too.

Just as she was walking off the ferry, she heard a man conversing with a woman who was probably his wife, as they jumped into their red Subaru that was parked along the curb. He remarked that the dead man had a couple of nasty gashes in his neck; that it possibly happened when he fell overboard. However, there was no blood on the body. They figured it was washed away by the water.

Mona sighed. "Oh well!" At least, the incident had taken all thoughts of suicide away. She considered then that maybe things did happen for a reason. For now, her thoughts remained on the mysteriously handsome stranger that had stood by her on the ferry.

Even in the chilling wind and wet, there had been a powerful presence about him. Whoever he was, she knew she would not forget him. What's more, she hoped she would see him again.

Normally, she didn't take the ferry this late. She had to walk a block and a half to her apartment – had been hers and Darren's – alone. Some areas along the strip were well-lit, but there were people from all stations of life around. Some stood around singing and playing guitars or mandolins, hoping for money to be dropped in their cups. Others merely observed, while the rest went on about their tasks of shopping in the variety of little stores at Pike Place Market, or rushing home from work. She was also more than aware of the lowlife that lurked in the shadows and around the backdoors of the numerous establishments. She walked as fast a pace as she could, doing her best not to run, not wanting anyone to know she was afraid of being alone.

At last, she came to Butler's Drug, where she rushed in through the front door, causing the bell overhead to ding-a-ling. She bid Harry Butler, the slightly overweight, middle-aged man with thinning dark hair – also the proprietor and her landlord – a quick hello and pushed her way through the door behind the drug department. She then hurried up the steep stairwell, where her footfalls echoed sharply, to the long hall and past three apartments until she reached the third, hers and Darren's. What had been hers and Darren's.

Sure enough, Darren was inside, handsome as ever with his clean-cut ash-blond hair and deep-set hazel eyes that could make her heart skip a beat, but he had his suitcase packed and his laptop closed, lying on the small beige sofa. He walked out of the bedroom, saw her, held his palms up in her face and quickly told her he didn't want to get into any further discussion. It was over and that was it.

"Can't you at least tell me why? Don't I deserve that much?"

He blew out air in obvious exasperation. "Mona, can't you just accept that it is over? I don't love you anymore. I thought I made that clear this afternoon. That is why I have been so distant with you the last couple of weeks. I don't want to go over it again!" He snatched up his suitcase and laptop. "Nancy's waiting for me," he admitted. "I'm moving in with her."

Her jaw dropped. Nancy was her best friend. Or so she had thought, in spite of the fact that Nancy was a little shallow. "Nancy Mullen?" she was incredulous.

"It's not the way you think, Mona. Nancy feels badly about this. She thinks a lot of you."

Mona guffawed disdainfully. "I bet she does!" All she felt besides utter and complete betrayal was rage. *"Oh my God!"*

He hurried out and slammed the door, while she stood there literally vibrating with anger. She growled like an animal at the top of her lungs and rushed out after him, running down the stairs, following him through the drugstore, past Harry and towards the street, where he jumped in the passenger side of Nancy's silver Volvo and slammed his door shut. She stepped off the curb, trying to grab the door handle just as they took off, and suddenly realized car lights were rushing towards her. She froze. Then someone grabbed her from behind and yanked her back on the sidewalk just as it flew by. She stood there in shock, staring at the traffic rushing by, trying to understand what had just happened.

"That was a very foolish thing to do, young lady," a strangely familiar voice with an accent said.

It finally hit her that she had been saved from certain death and she slowly turned and met those black pools again. She stood there speechless, shaking uncontrollably, staring up into mesmerizing depths.

Harry dashed out of the drugstore, arms flailing, anxiously inquiring if she was okay and then turned to the stranger. "Thank God you were here!"

The stranger smiled with a slight quirk of his lips.

Harry asked Mona if she was okay.

Ingesting her situation, she managed a yes nod.

Harry laid a hand on her shoulder. "You should come on in. I'll have Matilda fix you a cup of hot chocolate." His eyes went to the stranger. "Thank you! Thank you so much for saving Mona here.

God! I hate to think what would have happened had you not been near."

"Just doing the right thing," the low-pitched but euphonic voice replied.

"Tell you what," Harry said. "You need anything we carry in our establishment, you just let me know. It's yours for free."

"That's not necessary," he replied, smiling at Mona and then back to Mr. Butler. "Just take care of Mona here. That's all I ask." He went to walk away.

"Oh, we will certainly do that, Mr.—."

"Conta," he replied, turning around. "Count Gavril Conta...However, you may simply call me Gavril."

Mona's eyes grew big with surprise. "You're a...Count?"

"That I am," he replied with a polite nod. "I am from Romania. Arrived in Seattle early this evening."

"You were on the ferry," Mona stated.

"Ah! You remember," he said, looking pleased. "After I arrived, I didn't want to look for a place to stay, as yet." He smiled as though to himself. "Perhaps that was foolish of me, but I decided to ride the ferry. In fact, I made a couple of rounds by the time I saw you."

"Harry Butler here," the druggist interjected.

"A pleasure to meet you, Mr. Butler," Gavril said, shaking the druggist's hand.

"Same here."

Harry released Gavril's hand and took Mona by the arm to lead her to the door, but still addressed Gavril, "So you two met before?"

"Correct."

Mona spoke, "Yes. We were both on the ferry when some man jumped overboard." She looked at Gavril. "But you went inside when they were pulling the man out of the water."

"That's right. I did." He nodded politely. "Well, you drink your hot chocolate and try not to dash out in front of any more cars."

She felt herself flush. "I won't. Promise. Hey...I owe you my life."

He winked and then nodded respectfully to Harry, swiftly turned on his heels and disappeared into a throng of people on the sidewalk.

Once inside, Harry led Mona up to his apartment and had Matilda, who was inside cooking their dinner, take Mona in and make her some hot chocolate. He returned to the drugstore.

Matilda wasn't a very attractive woman, middle-aged and a little dumpy with mousy-brown hair, but her sweet personality made up for what she lacked in looks. She was at once concerned for Mona, making her the hot chocolate and then setting the pot of chili she was cooking on low, before sitting down to lend a sympathetic ear to Mona's woes.

Mona sat for several minutes sipping on her hot chocolate, going over the events of the past few hours. "I can't believe I almost killed myself stepping out in front of an oncoming car because of Darren! Jeeze! I'm such an idiot!"

"There…There, hon," Matilda said, patting Mona's hand lightly. "You're not an idiot. That Darren is a jerk and you deserve so much better than him. I never said this before, but I had a gut-feeling about him when you two first rented the apartment. I could see how foolish you were over him, though, and I hoped I was wrong."

"Really?" Mona inquired, gazing over the rim of her cup.

"Really. He just looked like a jerk to me."

It suddenly hit her. "Dammit! I can't show my face at work tomorrow! Darren and Nancy both will be there. I can just see everyone in the office whispering about me behind my back."

Matilda blew out air. "Hon! Now you've done nothing wrong! They are the ones who have something to be ashamed of. Not you!"

"Still…They've probably been seeing one another behind my back for weeks now. Everyone else has probably known about it for a while."

"Like I said, Mona. You walk in that office and hold your pretty honey blonde head high. You pay them no heed, other than to look at them as though they are the scum they are." Matilda poured herself a cup of chocolate and sat down by Mona. "Isn't Nancy the secretary of that young lawyer?"

"Yes she was, but she just got—."

"Promoted?" Matilda finished for her.

"Oh shit! That little worm! She pretended to be my friend, all the while getting her claws into Darren. Now she's Darren's secretary!"

"And Darren Graves is the son of Michael Graves."

"Yes! Head of the firm." Mona sat her now empty cup down.

"Want more, hon?"

"No. I'm good. Thanks, though." Her hands trembled. She clenched them into fists and relaxed them several times.

Matilda noticed. "Let me get you something a bit stronger than hot chocolate. What do you say? I have some Smirnoff and Sprite."

Mona nodded. "Yes. I'm not going anywhere else tonight. Make it a double shot."

"Coming right up."

Gavril moved slowly and carefully through the crowd mulling in and out of Pike Place Market. He stopped for a moment at the seafood display to observe men in soiled white aprons toss a salmon down to the end of the counter, where it was wrapped and handed over to a Hispanic woman in her forties. She paid for the fish and went on her way. Gavril smiled to himself as though he found it a bit amusing and moved on. He was thirsty, very thirsty. He had not fed on a live human in a couple of days, and now the maddening thirst was beginning to get the better of him. Had he been a younger and less experienced vampire, he would not have made it this long without feeding, but over his five hundred plus years, he had learned to control the powerful urges. Well, most of the time. Wasn't always the case when he was pissed. It had been all he could do not to grab the pretty young woman with hair the color of honeycombs and quench his thirst on her, but he liked her. There was something about her that had caught his attention when he noticed her back on the ferry. He sensed an unusual wild streak, even though he doubted that she knew it yet. It was there, though. He could smell it, and he found it titillating.

His thoughts turned to the man who had jumped overboard and drowned. The man had been contemplating suicide when Gavril noticed him by the ferry rail; one leg swung over, trying to follow through with his intentions. Gavril had silently zipped up to him and grabbed him long enough to wound him. Only the horrified man somehow managed to escape Gavril's grip and flung himself overboard. Someone from the bridge noticed the big splash as he fell into the water, and searchlights were instantly focused to the water. Gavril had no choice but to make himself less conspicuous, pulling back into the shadows. That was when he noticed Mona, looking so vulnerable, but beautiful and all alone, standing by the rail. Though thirsty, he wanted to get to know this human better, and had deliberately made himself known to her.

His thoughts turned to the present. Pedestrians were unloading from one of the car ferries that had just docked. Gavril noticed a sturdy looking young man, early to mid-twenties, talking excitedly on his cell phone about some concert he was headed to, but he wanted to get a coffee from Starbuck's first. There was a long line of customers waiting to order their coffees, so the young man decided to run into the market and then headed down a short hall to one of the bathrooms. That was when Gavril saw his chance, following the young man into the bathroom and, having assured himself that there was no one else in the bathroom, he waited quietly while the young man relieved himself. Soon as he stepped out to wash his hands, Gavril grabbed him and, stifling the young man's screams with one hand, he quickly fed from him, draining him to the point of passing out and then shimmered out with him, leaving him propped up against the outside back wall of a bar. There, Gavril picked up an empty whiskey bottle that lay beside a dumpster, broke it, smeared some of the young man's blood on it and placed the man's fingers of his right hand around the bottle's neck. He knew it probably wouldn't completely fool any doctor, but it would delay their focus on the real problem for a while. He was pretty sure that Seattle, in spite of their popularity in movies and television, hadn't had any genuine vampires hanging around in a long time. Done, he shimmered back to Starbucks and bought himself a mocha while visions of the lovely Mona filled his head. The next thing he knew, he was walking towards the drugstore where she lived in an apartment overhead. He hadn't forgotten the druggist's offer. He didn't need anything from the drugstore, but perhaps the man had a vacant apartment for rent.

Harry was more than happy to rent the apartment across the hall and down a few feet to the left from Mona's. After Gavril paid his first month's rent and had the key, he returned to the ferry terminal and retrieved his small suitcase from a locker he had rented, and then hurried back to the apartment. At least, he could rest assured that his casket, the one he had crossed over in on a Swedish cargo vessel, was stashed away safely in a storage unit close to the docks. He had paid for six months storage in advance. If he were to decide to stay any longer, he would pay the difference.

Once inside his apartment, he set the suitcase on the bed and put away the few things he had brought with him. Money was not a problem. He was filthy rich, having inherited much wealth from his family earlier on, investing it wisely in various stocks and such. A new suit, a couple of pairs of designer jeans, some shirts and underwear were chickenfeed to him. Then he retrieved the bottle of wine from the inside pocket of his trench coat. He'd picked it up from a liquor store, along with a bottle of Jack Daniels, before it closed.

Unpacking accomplished, he poured himself a glass of wine and relaxed back on the brown leather, easy chair that came furnished with the apartment. It was a little torn here and there, but it was clean. The whole apartment was immaculate. Though it was a simple abode, it would do for now.

He took a sip of the wine and leaned his head back, closing his eyes. For some reason, his thoughts turned back in time to Alina Banica, the first woman he had ever loved. He had not thought of her in years. One reason being, her death and what had followed had been so painful to him that he had purposely pushed the memories of it all back into his subconscious.

Alina had been a servant girl in Dracula's castle. Gavril had been smitten by her from the age of sixteen, when she was only twelve, but because of social standards, the elite did not openly mix with peasantry. He left her alone, but for years, he admired the girl, but kept his distance. Still, as he grew older, the girl became even more beautiful. Eventually, he could not keep his attraction to her a secret from his cousin anymore, and told him of his feelings. He had even remained single, because of his desire for her.

Dracula found Gavril's crush somewhat amusing, even encouraged Gavril to have his way with her, if he so desired. Gavril had been happy with this, and the young woman was apparently interested, confessing she had always liked him too. Only Gavril's feelings for the young woman grew too serious and his cousin did not like this, and took the young woman for himself to – as he put it – teach Gavril a lesson. Even knowing full well that his cousin could rip him to shreds, Gavril went into a rage and challenged him. Dracula would not be challenged, not by kin. In front of Gavril's eyes, Dracula ripped the young woman's throat out and drank her dry, killing her immediately.

The horrified Gavril fell to his knees and swore that he would find a way to kill him. His words were no sooner uttered, and Dracula attacked him, and drank from him to the point of death, then fed him his own blood. At which time, he killed Gavril and placed him in his cold dark dungeon in a casket beside his own. Gavril then awoke later that very evening, horrified he had been laid in a casket, and then seeing his cousin's casket beside his, quickly realized that he too was now a monster.

Gavril's mind snapped back to the present. Why had he remembered that now? He pondered for several minutes before it hit – Mona! Mona reminded him of Alina, with hair the color of honey; her slightly turned up nose, and big blue eyes. In fact, she was practically her doppelganger. He felt something wet trickle down his cheek and reached up with his forefinger. A tear. He was crying. He stood immediately and placed his empty glass in the sink. Perhaps he should go for a long walk. He shrugged into his black trench coat and left. He was glad the Butler's had retired for the evening, as he didn't feel like exchanging pleasantries. Unlocking the front door with the key Harry had furnished, he left.

Nancy Mullen stepped out of the shower, wrapped a yellow towel around her long, golden brown hair and stared into the steam-clouded mirror and wiped a circle clean with her hand to see herself. That was when she heard Darren crack open the door. "Come on in. You're late. I've already showered," she said, turning and smiling wickedly up into his hazel eyes. She locked her fingers behind his neck and pressed her still warm and wet naked body up to his.

He didn't seem to mind getting his shirt and pants wet. "Darn. I was hoping to step in with you."

"Sorry. I used up all the hot water." She bit softly into his bottom lip and then kissed him fully.

He mumbled something incoherent and pulled her tightly against him. She cooed. With no further coaxing, he swept her up into his arms and carried her to their bed, quickly tossing his tie, shirt and pants aside as he undressed. Seconds later, they were going at it hot and heavy on top of the bedcovers. She giggled as they rolled over in the bed, placing her on top, his favorite position. "How did Mona take it?" she asked as she worked him for all she was worth.

"Not well," he breathlessly replied. "She's sweet but not my type."

"Am I your type?" she asked; eyes now focused on his half-moon birthmark just above his right nipple.

"Damn right!" he hotly answered, reaching his peak. "Damn right!"

"Right answer," she said and sped up her moves, meeting both their needs. She happily yelled out then as they finished together. She laid there for a few seconds, letting them both cool down and then rolled off, jumped off the bed, grinning mischievously.

"What?" he inquired.

"I think we soiled the new comforter."

He jumped up too and assessed the damage to the powder blue comforter. "Hell. It'll wash. There's another one in the top of the closet."

She gathered up the bottom ends of the comforter and, with his help, they folded it up and tossed it over in the far corner.

"The water should be hot again," she suggested.

"Good. Now we can shower together and then go eat. I know we eat there a lot, but does Olive Garden sound okay?"

"Perfect. I'm starving. You know me. I never tire of their salads."

It was all Mona could do to hold it together the next morning when she walked into the front office of Graves & Sons. She could feel the stares burning into the back of her head as she disappeared down the hall and into Michael Graves' office. Michael Graves was the senior member of the firm and Darren's father. He had taken her on as his private secretary the past week, which thrilled her at the time, before Darren burst her bubble. Though he had been married, not necessarily happy, for over twenty-five years, Mona could tell he was interested. She, too, found him very attractive for an older man, but it was his son Darren who had ripped her heart out. There was no doubt that Michael knew. It was in his hooded gray eyes as she walked in the door. "Morning, Mona," he said, eyeing her intuitively.

"Morning, Michael." Shortly after he had promoted her to be his personal secretary, he had let her know that when they were in his office, he would prefer her to call him Michael, that formalities could be left to the courtroom and during meetings.

"Could you get me the Brandenburg file?"

"Certainly. Soon as I put my purse up."

"Thank you."

She glanced at his half empty coffee mug. "Would you like a refill, too?"

"That would be awesome. But take your time."

She offered him a simple smile. He was being extra nice this morning. It was kind of him, but what she really wanted to do was run out of there and keep on running, just as far and just as fast as her legs would take her.

She brought him the file and poured him fresh coffee. He politely thanked her and indicated with a nod for her to sit down while he went over the file. "You know," he said after a few minutes, "I firmly believe Rick Harrison is innocent."

The name caught her off guard, as he was looking at the Brandenburg file. "Rick Harrison, Michael?"

"You know the man charged with brutally raping a fifteen-year-old teenage girl last week."

"Yes! I remember now. The media's having a field day with that one."

Chin lowered, he peered up at her from over his reading glasses. "Don't they always?"

"Doesn't he have a court-appointed attorney? A public defender?"

Michael nodded in the affirmative and took a long slow sip of his coffee before placing his mug on the desk. He read for a few more minutes and then closed the file and set it aside, focusing on her. "I got this idiot – not Rick, another guy – off Scott free last year, but I know he's guilty as sin." He smiled pensively. "But that's why I'm wealthy, isn't it? I get the crooks with money off, while the innocent get locked away because they don't have the money for the right representation."

All this was new to Mona. She had always thought highly of Michael, but this was enlightening. He was coming out and admitting the not-always-so-pretty truth of things.

"Don't look so shocked, Mona." He leaned back in his chair, placing entwined fingers behind his head. "Like that no good, two-timing son of mine. God knows I love him. He's my son. But he's rotten to the core."

Mona was slack-jawed; hearing Michael admit what everyone else knew but was hesitant to vocalize.

His voice raised slightly, "It just pisses me off that he dumped you for Nancy...Not that she's not attractive, but she doesn't have what you do."

She cleared her throat. "What's that, Michael?"

Voice returning to normal, he replied, "What few of us have, Mona – integrity. You would have made him a good wife."

Not knowing what to say, she cleared her throat again.

"No doubt about it, he's a damn good lawyer. Probably better than I am, but he's just like his mother – selfish to the core."

Not sure how to respond, or even if she should, she simply bobbed her head.

"I want to do something I haven't done in a long time."

"What is that, sir?"

"Michael! Call me Michael."

"Sorry...I'm just a little—."

"Confused," he replied for her."

"Yes. That's it."

"I want you to find out all you can on this Rick Harrison. Get me a complete background check. Where he went to school. How long? Is he left-handed or right-handed? Does he cough loud or soft? Everything!"

"I'll get on it right away, Michael."

"If I still have this feeling after I go over everything, I am going to take up his case."

"You are?" As far as she knew, no one in the firm had ever offered their services to someone for free, without it being court-appointed.

"Damn right! I am sick and tired of what I see daily. It is about time someone did something nice for someone. More importantly, I want that sorry ass son of mine to witness an act of kindness in his meaningless existence."

Never had she seen Michael so determined or passionate about anything. His enthusiasm was inspiring. She stood. "I'll get on it right now, Michael."

"Thank you, Mona."

She exited through the door to her office, which was adjacent to his, but smaller.

"And I'm sorry."

She turned back around, sticking her head out the door. "What?"

"I am sorry Darren is doing what he is. I hate it! He's a fool."

She stood there for a few seconds. His statement brought tears to her eyes. "Thank you, Michael. That means a lot."

"It's true. Now you go dig up what you can on Harrison."

"Right!" Stifling back the tears, she went off to make phone calls.

Chapter Two:

Mona did a double-take when Rick Harrison was escorted into the bare, white-walled, visitation room by a burly, middle-aged officer with the name Pope on his badge. There was something strangely familiar about the prisoner – she'd never laid eyes on him in person before, just newspaper shots – still, he reminded her of someone, but she couldn't quite put her finger on whom. He was much younger looking than she had anticipated. Didn't look a day over twenty-five, but she knew he was in his late thirties. "Five minutes, Ms. Sims," the officer informed.

"I know. Michael Graves just wanted me to ask Mr. Harrison a few questions."

"Like I said. Five minutes." He held up five fingers.

Harrison reluctantly settled back in his chair, eyeing Mona suspiciously with almost yellow eyes. "I take it Michael Graves is an attorney?"

"Yes! And a good one."

That brought on an immediate sardonic laugh from Harrison. "Doesn't the Gilbert girl already have a lawyer?"

"Yes! Steve Bundleson is the prosecutor."

"What I thought…So, what could you possibly want with me?"

"Mr. Graves is interested in defending you?"

Harrison drew back his head, brow furrowed and a questioning stare.

"You heard me correctly."

"You're shittin' me." He shook his head and scooted around in his seat. "I don't get it. Why? I don't have any money. I'm just a poor mechanic. Work my ass off just to pay my rent and child support to my ex for our three girls."

"Teenagers, aren't they?"

"Yes. So?"

"All about the same age as the girl who claims you raped her."

"I suppose. Hadn't really thought about it."

"Michael…Mr. Graves, has been kind of interested in your case from the beginning."

He fidgeted around in his seat some more, eyeing her with reservation and distrust. "Why?"

"It just struck him as odd that a man in his late thirties with three teenage daughters of his own, with never having so much as a parking ticket against his name, would suddenly rape a teenage girl."

Harrison sighed and shrugged; expression noncommittal.

Mona studied him momentarily. "Well?"

"Well…what?"

"Are you guilty?"

He straightened in his chair and leaned forward, answering with an articulate, "Hell no!"

If Harrison was guilty, it wasn't showing in his demeanor. Mona believed him. "That's what I wanted to hear."

Harrison cocked his head sideways. "And?"

"If you're willing, consider yourself represented with one of the best criminal lawyers available, Mr. Harrison."

With consternation, Harrison's voice rose in pitch, "But I don't have a dime to pay him?"

"Doesn't matter. He wants to represent you. So, what do you say? You want to take your chances with the public defender? He's an okay lawyer. Or, do you want to be represented by one of the very best criminal lawyers around?"

Harrison scooted back his chair and stood. "I don't trust this. Why should I believe you? You settin' me up for some kind of trap?"

"No!" Mona stood too and her eyes went to the door, as Officer Pope entered the room.

"Time's up," Pope stated with a harsh edge to his tone.

"Please, Rick!" Mona pleaded. "Please believe me. This is no joke…No setup. Mr. Graves really wants to defend you."

Pope took hold of Harrison's arm.

Harrison eyed Mona, eyes searching. A downed man wanting to survive, but until a few minutes prior had given up. "This is really on the up and up?"

"Yes!" Mona assured him.

"Okay…Don't let me down."

Mona blew out air in relief. "We won't. Mr. Graves will be in touch with you shortly."

Harrison's head bobbed and one could almost see the wheels turning behind those yellow eyes that seemed so familiar but difficult to place. "Thank you!" he replied and went with Pope out of the room.

With more errands to run for Michael, it was noon by the time Mona arrived back at the office building. Michael walked out of the glass doors just as she was about to enter. "You deliver the message to Harrison?"

"Sure did. First thing."

"How'd he react?" he asked, as he held onto his hat to keep it on his head. A strong wind had blown up suddenly.

"Dubious, at first. But I think he would really like to have you represent him."

"Good! I have a couple of stops to make, but I hope to run by and see him."

"Oh? I thought you were on your way to lunch."

He let go of his hat, as the wind settled momentarily. "I ate a quick sandwich." He shook his head thoughtfully. "Got a nagging feeling about this case, Mona. Been a long time since I had this kind of feeling in my gut." He chuckled lightly. "Who knows…Maybe I'm just a crazy aging, has-been lawyer. Maybe this will be the end of my career. Gads!"

"I think you are far from being a has-been, Michael. You're still the best criminal lawyer in the county."

He smiled amiably and gently touched her shoulder. "That's why I wanted you to be my personal secretary, Mona. You have a heart." He glanced at his watch. "Got to go now. You get yourself some lunch…On me!" He stuck his hand in his wallet and pulled out two twenties.

"That's kind of you, Michael. But you don't need to pay for my lunch."

"I want to. Now take it." He folded the bills in her hand, winked and swiftly walked off towards the parking garage.

Mona stared down at the two twenties. One was more than enough, as she usually just had a salad. "Oh…well," she sighed and went on inside.

It was good dark, after eight, when Gavril heard what he instantly recognized as the clickety-clicking of Mona's high heels coming up the stairs. He, himself, had been home only a few minutes. A vague hint of a smile creased the corners of his mouth. Although he had moved in the apartment across and diagonal from hers the night before, she had retired for the night early, and hadn't been aware that he was there. He left his door closed, as he wasn't about to do something so obvious as to rush out and greet her. No. He would just tidy up his small kitchen a bit more and enjoy listening to her move around. His acute hearing far exceeded that of mere mortals, and he could hear a pin drop behind her closed door. He could also smell her from where he was. She had an especially lovely scent: Her own natural body odor mingled nicely with a light scent of juniper. He supposed it was her perfume. It was refreshingly different, reminded him of the outdoors. Suited her well.

Over the years he had grown very picky about the females he chose to be possible mates. Most women just did not have what he deemed essential in making a good vampire mate. He wanted a mate to spend eternity with, couldn't afford for her to have too many flaws. However, there had been three in the last two hundred years. Unfortunately, he had ended up killing each one because they could not learn to control their thirst for blood. He wanted a mate, a lover, longed for one, but not one who would carelessly bring their presence to the attention of the public.

Still, he had all the time in the world, so there was no need to hurry. He was willing to court the lovely Mona first, if it was necessary, to gain her trust; a must, if she was going to let him turn her willingly; and willingly was the key factor. He wanted his mate to truly love him, not just love him because he hypnotized her to, which he could do with great ease. He was exceptionally good-looking, irresistible to the opposite sex, when he wanted to be, as all vampires were; what few there were around. Most of them were in Europe, but he knew of some that had come to the US.

He had spent the day inside, as the sun had been out bright, but soon as it was dark enough, he had ventured out for a short time, not tarrying too long, as he wanted to be home when Mona was there.

There were times when he could risk a daylight outing, when it was heavily clouded over, but it hadn't been today. There was a small television furnished with the apartment, of which he was grateful. He hadn't really expected that much from such a small place. When he wasn't watching pedestrians on the sidewalk below, some rushing in and out of the drugstore, he was watching television or cleaning. Although there wasn't much cleaning to be done. Even though the paint on the walls had seen better days and the furniture had an antique flavor, the apartment was pretty neat, neater than many of the various abodes he had occupied over the centuries, when he wasn't staying in his own castle back in Romania. Not Bran castle, but a relatively new one, that he had built for himself some fifty years prior, which was pretty much a replica of Poenari Castle. (Sometimes sentiment got the best of him.) Though it wasn't the original, it was as much like the old one that was possible to replicate, dungeon and all.

After returning back to his apartment, he had cleaned some more, but now, bored with cleaning, he relaxed in supine position on his bed, staring up at the light-brown stains on the old ceiling – what had once been white – wallpaper. Yes, the apartment had seen better days. Still, it was clean and neat and that was what counted. Although he liked nice things, he'd been around far too many years to let trivial things like luxury matter to him. Sufficient was good enough. The apartment served its purpose.

He lay there for a good half hour simply enjoying the sounds of Mona moving around in her apartment. She had made herself a sandwich and settled down to eat and watch television. He could tell all of this with his acute senses. A few minutes later, there were more footsteps coming up the stairs, heavier more labored footsteps – Harry Butler. He knocked respectfully on Mona's door.

Inside, Mona sat her plate down and answered, speaking with surprise to see her landlord there. Normally, he didn't drop by to check on her, but because of the incident the evening before, he stated that he had been concerned about her all day and wanted to see how she was doing. She let him know that she was doing just fine and offered to make him a glass of iced tea, and invited him to come in, but he politely declined and said that Matilda had supper ready. He went to walk away, but then turned in his tracks and asked her if she'd seen Mr. Conta yet.

"Actually…no," she answered mildly surprised. "Why? Have you seen him?"

"Yesterday evening… He moved in the vacant apartment."

Her eyes swiveled to the neighboring door. "Oh! You mean he's our neighbor now?"

"That he is. Remember I told him that anything in the store was his? Just to name it?"

"Yes. I remember, vaguely."

"Well, he came back later and told me he needed a place to stay and wondered if I had anything. I let him know the apartment was available… even though we haven't kept it up as well as we have yours." There was a note of apology in his voice. "But he seemed happy to get it. So, he's our new neighbor now."

"That's good. Thanks for telling me. I would definitely have been surprised to bump into him up here, had you not told me."

"Yes. That occurred to me. I thought it was the least I could do for him, since he saved your life."

"I appreciate your letting me know."

"Well, I'd better get going. Matilda doesn't like it when I let supper get cold."

"Okay, Mr. Butler.

"Harry, Mona…Call me Harry."

"All right, Harry." She thanked him again for coming up to see about her and he left. Smiling to herself – he reminded her of Michael, insisting she call him by his first name – she softly closed her door.

Eyes half-shut, Gavril sat there grinning to himself as he listened to Harry's heavy footfalls echoing down the hall to his and his wife's own apartment, which was considerably larger. Gavril could tell by the acoustics of the building. He lay there for a while longer, and soon heard water running in Mona's bathroom. She was taking a shower. His slight smile grew larger as he imagined her lovely nude body being sprayed with the warm water. His inclination was to jump up from the bed and rush in to shower with her. But that certainly would not work. For one, he would scare her half to death and get himself evicted from the apartment. That is, if he didn't kill everyone first. Something he would have done in his earlier days as a vampire. As powerful as his desire was to press himself up against her lovely, enticingly wet, body, it would have to wait. Besides, he preferred to earn her complete and absolute trust.

Mona stepped out of the shower, grabbed her large yellow towel that hung over the glass shower door and toweled off. Her thoughts had not been of Darren as they had been earlier. Throughout her shower, all she could think of was Count Gavril Conta living so close by. She wondered if he were home. Would she see him soon? Would she see him often? Or just once in a while? Surely he had a job. She had no clue what he did. He looked much too sophisticated to be living in an apartment such as she and he were living. That in itself was strange and something to seriously ponder. He was so…mysterious, not only in his looks, but in his actions. Surely he could afford someplace much nicer than here. As far as that went, she could too.

She and Darren had originally rented this place together, thinking they would be there only a short time. Only it ended up being much longer. She wondered about that as well. Now, she realized that the reason Darren had not suggested they move into a better class place was because he had no intentions of staying with her! She sniggered sarcastically to herself. "I am such a dupe!"

Back in Gavril's apartment, he whispered, "No you're not, Mona. It is Darren who is the dupe. I will prove it to you."

Not quite ready to settle into bed for the night, even though she had to rise early in the morning, had to be at the office by seven, as she promised to get some legwork done for Michael before settling down to their daily routine of appointments, hearings, and luncheons, Mona slipped into a clean pair of jeans and a dark blue sweatshirt, clothes she normally wore when just hanging around her apartment, and settled down in front of the television again to watch the late news.

A male African American reporter stood in the pounding rain in a yellow raincoat, excitedly giving what details he could of two mysterious deaths in the last few hours. A man and a woman, apparently not related, had been found by the ferry dock, and had succumbed to a great loss of blood. It appeared that their throats had been ripped out by some, unidentified animal. There were speculations that it was a large, rabid dog. However, the police weren't giving out much information at this point. They had come from different families and had not known one another.

In his own apartment, Gavril poured himself a shot of Smirnoff and drank it down, all the while, smiling roguishly to himself. He had thought of venturing out again, still a little thirsty for blood, as he had not quite quenched it, but he had decided to wait. He was instantly glad he had made the decision to stay, for he heard the steps of a man coming up the stairwell. It wasn't Butler either. He could tell by the squeak of the man's shoes that they were expensive leather. There was no doubt in his mind that the man was on his way up to see Mona. Gavril waited patiently for each footfall until the man stopped at Mona's door and knocked impatiently.

The secretive smile Gavril normally wore transformed to the more sadistic. If this man was a threat to Mona at all, perhaps he could have him for desert?

Mona jumped up. "Who in hell—?" For a brief moment, she hoped it was Gavril Conta, but then she realized that he probably would not be knocking on her door this late. It was almost eleven. She opened the door a crack. "Darren!"

"Hi, Mona."

"What are *you* doing here? Nancy ditch your sorry ass?"

That seemed to amuse him, as he snorted a laugh. "Of course not. Just thought I'd drop by and see how you're doing."

"I'm fine, Darren! It's late and I don't care to talk to you."

He stuck his foot in the door before she could shut it. "Aw come on. I just want to talk a minute."

"Why? You don't care about me. You just led me on these past few months. Let me think we had a future together, and all the while you were screwing Nancy."

He shoved on the door, almost knocking her down, and walked in past her.

Spinning around, she angrily stated, "You're *not* welcome here!"

He faced her, expression instantly transforming to the apologetic. "Hey…I just don't want hard feelings."

"Right. You just damn near knocked me to the floor!"

He exhaled heavily. "Sorry. I didn't mean to shove the door that hard. Look…I really did not want to hurt you. In the beginning, I really did want to be with you."

Her face contorted; everything within her telling her not to believe a word he said, yet part of her wanted to believe him. "All right. What is it that you have to say?"

"That's more like it." His face softened and he stepped up to her. "I see my dad has taken you in as his private secretary now."

"That's right. It's been several days. You're just now noticing?"

"No. I noticed the first day." He glanced down at his shoes momentarily and then back up to her, his eyes meeting hers. "You know my dad really likes you?"

"I'm very aware of that Darren."

"I mean he *really* likes you. He and Mom have stayed together all these years, but they quit loving one another a long time ago. She stays with him for the money and prestige. And God only knows why he stays with her."

"Maybe he still cares about her, Darren?"

"Right," he answered with a contemptuous laugh.

Rolling her eyes, she went to step away from him, but he grabbed her suddenly and kissed her.

Infuriated, she shoved him away. "What the hell did you do that for?"

He wiped off his mouth with the sleeve of his shirt. "I'm not really sure. Guess I wanted to see if I still felt anything for you."

She grimaced as she thought about his actions. Then it was suddenly clear to her. "You little piece of shit – You're jealous!"

He chortled, amused. "Me? Jealous? Of my *dad?*"

"Why in hell else would you come here? You're actually afraid your father and I might get together. And it *bothers* you."

Though he shook his head, he didn't vocally deny it.

"I want you to go, Darren."

He didn't budge, just stared.

She went to the door that was still open. "Please! Go!"

He maintained his stance. It was obvious he wasn't sure what he wanted anymore.

"You're with Nancy now, Darren. And there is nothing between your father and me other than friendship and respect. Respect! Do you even have a clue what that is?"

His head bobbed slightly. Still, he hesitated.

"Please go…" she said more softly this time.

He suddenly cut a stare to something in the hall.

She snapped her head around to see – Gavril Conta stood there; piercing eyes fixed on Darren, black as midnight and unmoving. Chills shot up her spine and she could have sworn Darren shuddered.

"This man bothering you, Mona?" Gavril asked in a low voice that resonated with eerie clarity and resolve – No man was going to cross him.

There was an audible gulp from Darren, and he wasn't about to stick around to argue. Eyes back to Mona, he muttered, "I'm sorry." He fled out the door and down the hall, glancing back only once at Gavril, who had not moved his black eyes off him.

Mona was mesmerized. Never had she been so thrilled with fear and awe at the same time. At that moment, Gavril was the most fascinating, yet, the most attractive, and the most striking man she'd ever laid eyes on. Yet, he terrified her very soul. She couldn't decide if she wanted to run from or to him; for something within her feared that if she ran to him that she would be his slave forever. He turned his gaze to her then, and he didn't have to say a word. She was so caught up in those sparkling, obsidian depths that she could not move, could not breathe, she was completely and utterly paralyzed.

In a whisper, he was before her. "Breathe, Mona."

She caught her breath, sucking in air. "Oh God!" She found she could not move her eyes from his.

"Don't fear me, Mona," he said, speaking in that low, soft voice that was clear and crisp as an ice sculpture and even more enthralling. "It is *not* my desire to ever harm you."

Her head quivered and her legs suddenly felt like ropes. It was all she could do to remain standing.

"I think that perhaps you should go inside now. I do not believe your friend will be back tonight, but if he does…he'd better have good reason. Or he just might regret it."

"Yes. I'll…I'll go in. Need to get up early."

He winked, smiled that surreptitious smile and stepped backwards into his apartment and ever so slowly closed his door.

Not having his eyes locked on hers anymore, she found the strength to move and returned to her apartment as well. She leaned, collapsed, back against her door. "Oh God! What just happened?"

Nancy heard someone at the door, fumbling, attempting to unlock it. Her brow creased, puzzled. Whoever it was either didn't have a key or was having trouble. "Darren?"

Only mumbling expletives coming from the other side.

"What the—?"

Then the knob jiggled and Darren finally made his way in, dropping his briefcase in the floor and tripping over it. His hair was in disarray and he was chalk-white, brow beading sweat.

"My God!" She rushed up to him, retrieving the briefcase for him and tossing it on the coffee table. "Darren? Crap! What happened?"

His look was pitiful, dazed, as though he'd been drugged. "I…I'm not sure."

"Did you fall and hit your head?"

"No…Don't think so," he replied, still confused.

"Did you drive your car home?"

He managed to straighten, squaring his shoulders, blinking, trying to clear his thoughts. "I must have." He looked down at his right hand. It held his keys.

"Oh my God! I think I should take you to the hospital."

"No!" he replied, shaking his head vigorously. "I… I will be okay… Maybe I did hit my head or something."

"All the more reason for me to take you."

"Coffee…Is there coffee made?"

"Sure. I'll get you some right now."

"Good!" He collapsed down on the sofa while she went to get his coffee. Squeezing his temples with his palms, he tried to remember exactly what had happened. He had gone to see Mona. That much he remembered. And he didn't want Nancy to know." His head throbbed, pulse pounding through his temples. "Babe?"

"Yes," she called from the kitchen.

"Can you bring me a couple of Tylenol?"

"I'll get them right now."

Black eyes! Yes. He remembered cold black eyes, the depths of which he'd never seen, nor did he wish to see again. A man, a foreigner, had been standing in the hall in front of Mona's apartment. What he had seen in that man's eyes terrified him to the very core. Normally, little got to him, let alone scared him. He was spoiled and didn't hesitate to admit it, used to getting his way. Tonight, though, had been a wakeup call. There was something or someone in this world that could get to him, someone who petrified his very soul. If he never saw the man again, it would be too soon. "God help me!"

Nancy was back. "What, Darren?" She handed him his Tylenol and a cup of coffee.

"Nothing," he muttered, thanked her and took the pills, chucking them down first, and following them with a sip of coffee. He forced himself to lean back and tried to smile; although he was pretty sure it wasn't very convincing. He had to tell Nancy something. "I almost got hit by a car after I parked mine. Wasn't paying attention." He broadened his fake smile. "Was in a hurry to get home to you."

"Oh! My poor Darren!" She dropped down beside him, hugging and kissing his cheek, attempting to comfort him.

He did appreciate her gesture, but he knew that nothing in this world would ever help him forget that man and the way he had looked at him. *Nothing!* He still wasn't sure how he got home. As disoriented and confused as he felt, he was amazed he was still alive.

Gavril waited until Mona was fast asleep before he slipped quietly out of the building. It was close to midnight when he made his way to Pike Place Market. Most decent folk had gone home by now, but there were still a few straggling couples here and there, lingering on the sidewalks and in front of the stores, some holding hands and talking while they aimlessly walked about. Others were further back in the shadows, making out in the nooks and crannies between the establishments. Then there were the homeless, wandering around looking for a scrap here and there in any back alley dumpster they could find. He stepped over more than one wino passed out, leaning up against the back wall of a building.

He could have fed on any of them, but he didn't want to feed on just anyone. He noticed an attractive, middle-aged woman, alluringly dressed in a very short red skirt and her healthy bosom practically hanging out of her white sleeveless top. Very skimpy attire for the cool air. Her hair was black and pulled back in a long pony tail, and she wore big silver hoop earrings. She was leaning over, talking to a man in a car that had pulled over to the curb. No doubt, she was a hooker. He decided to see if the man was going to pick her up or not. Apparently, she was too expensive for the man's taste, so he drove off. She flipped him the bird and stepped back, looking around, hoping another prospect would pull up.

Gavril saw his opportunity, stepping up behind the woman. "I take it you're free for the evening?" he inquired, startling her.

She spun around. "Jesus! You scared the shit out of me!"

"My sincere apologies, ma'am." He smiled his most contagious smile.

Instantly, she was enthralled. "Normally, a hundred dollars, up front." She ogled him over, apparently more than liking what she saw. "But for you, hon…Fifty."

"I can manage that."

"Awesome!" she slipped a slender hand in his. "My place is this way."

She led him a few buildings down, around a corner, through a back door and up a flight of stairs to the third floor, where her apartment was the second door on the right. She unlocked the door and held it open for Gavril to enter. Once inside, she proceeded to pull off her top, wasting no time. Gavril quietly removed his clothes too. She stood before him, naked, her big boobs with dark nipples beckoning.

In a breath, he was before her.

"How in hell did you move that fast? I didn't even see you move."

His reply was an amused grin. Then he hoisted her up in his arms, thrusting himself into her hard before she had time to anticipate him.

She let out a little cry of pain. "Hey…Not so rough."

He gripped her buttocks, holding her up with his hands and kissed her, all the while screwing her in an upright position and with a fierceness she'd never known before.

"Shit!" she cried out. "You're freakin' rough!"

"Want me to stop?" he asked, black eyes piercing hers.

She shivered. "…No! No! Don't stop!"

He had merely asked, but he had no intention of stopping. He worked her hard and feverishly, making her thrill and cry all at the same time.

"You're hurting me," she cried again. But then she begged for more. "Don't stop! Shit! Don't stop! I've never been screwed like this before. Never! Who are you?"

He slammed her down on the bed then, pushing her legs as far apart as they would go and drove himself in even deeper. She screamed this time. "Want me to stop?" he asked again, with no intentions of doing so. He was enjoying it too much. She was a whore, and he was going to give it to her like no other man could.

Tears were streaming down her face now. "You're hurting me," she cried again.

"Maybe this will help." He opened his mouth wide, letting his fangs protrude.

Horrified now, she let out a terrible scream, but it was to no avail. He clamped his fangs deep into her neck.

"Help me!" she cried out.

There was no one to hear, though. At least, no one that would care. That he was sure of. He was very thirsty and drank a lot of her blood, and would have drained her, but she kept begging him to stop. He decided to hell with it and released his bite. He stared down into her terrified brown eyes. For what it was worth, she was very pretty, and there was something about her that he liked. She was also, in spite of her pain, moving under him, still responding to his love-making.

"Want me to quit?" he asked mockingly, knowing that, in spite of her fear, she wanted him.

She managed a whisper. "No…Don't quit."

"Good girl!" he felt her coming around and he released with a fury, slamming away at her until she finished peaking, and then he held her tightly while they vibrated together.

Finished, he pulled out of her, stood, retrieved his clothing, and quietly began to dress.

Though greatly weakened, she managed to get up, and began to put on her clothes, as well. Her eyes kept darting to his, but then she would look away. Finally, she got the courage to ask, "You're a vampire, aren't you?"

"Yes I am," he answered with a wicked smile.

"I…I thought vampires weren't real." She gulped, and then she said, "Thank you for not killing me."

"Honestly, to kill or not kill you is neither here nor there with me. Killing is my nature." His eyes went to her neck. It had quit bleeding. His saliva was responsible for that.

"Then why did you stop when I begged you to?"

"I don't know. Maybe I felt sorry for you."

"Well, thank you anyway."

Fully dressed now, he reached in his pocket and pulled out his wallet. He handed a bill over to her. Her jaw dropped as she looked, unbelieving at the bill. Then she turned her eyes back to his. "Five hundred dollars! You're giving me five hundred dollars?"

"It was worth it. You're good at what you do. Go buy yourself something nice."

Her eyes misted over. "Thank you! Thank you!"

"Also, you might want to take some B-twelve vitamins and iron…to get your strength up."

"Yes…Yes…I'll do that. Thanks!"

Smiling surreptitiously, and with no further word, he vanished in front of her eyes.

Always thirsty for blood, Gavril searched for someone else to finish feeding on. He heard yelling. There was a big, burly African American male slapping a woman around in between a couple of buildings. Judging from what the woman was saying to the man, she was his girlfriend. She was crying hysterically and begging him to let her go. Gavril had the man by his throat before he even knew what hit him. Lunging back, the woman stood there screaming. Gavril released his bite on the man long enough to snarl, "Get out of here while you can! Or I'll have you for desert!"

She didn't have to be told twice, tore off down the alley, running for her life.

Gavril chuckled wickedly then and finished his meal, draining the man dry. At last, sated, he shimmered on back to his apartment.

To Mona's delight, she slept well, more sound than usual. She woke up the next morning full of energy, ready for work before she finished her first cup of coffee, when she normally drank down two. Without really thinking about what she was doing, she kept her ears peeled for sounds of Gavril coming out of his apartment. She assumed he had a job somewhere. Only, all was silent before and as she left for work. She figured he must have risen earlier than she.

"Oh well," she mumbled and headed on down the stairs. Harry and Matilda were both in the drugstore as she dashed through on her way out. They spoke cheerful hellos and she greeted back, equally so. Part of her wanted to ask Harry if he knew where Gavril worked, but she decided that that was being nosey and pushed the notion to the back of her mind.

Michael Graves closed his briefcase and raised his eyes to Rick Harrison, who sat across from him, subdued and hopeless. There was something familiar about Rick Harrison, but Michael couldn't quite determine what it was. "Rick," Michael said, setting down his briefcase, "I can't make any promises. I admit that right now things aren't looking real good for you."

Harrison barely nodded, staring down at the white, tiled floor.

"However, I promise you this. I will do my damdest to prove you innocent."

Harrison pinched the bridge of his nose and dropped his hand down, meeting eyes with the lawyer. "I am more than grateful that you have decided to defend me. Only for the life of me, I fail to understand why. Why are you defending me?"

"Didn't my secretary tell you?"

"Yes. She said something about you wanting to do the right thing for someone who couldn't afford representation. For someone you believe to be innocent. That brings me to ask – Why do you believe I am innocent?"

"Aren't you?"

"Yes!"

"That's why I believe you," Michael replied.

Harrison's forehead narrowed in confusion. "Huh?"

"Not a flinch. No hesitation in your response." He let out a little snort. "And, there's something not right here. I just feel it."

"Not quite sure I follow you, sir."

"Please, call me Michael."

Harrison's face relaxed marginally. "Okay…As I said, I am not quite sure I follow you, Michael."

"Look at it this way. I've been a lawyer for many years. I've represented a lot of not-so-innocent people. I can pretty much tell when someone is lying to me…even sociopaths. Though they can keep a poker face when lying their asses off, their eyes are cold as ice floes. What I saw in your eyes on television during the news, I see in your eyes now: pain…hurt…anger."

Listening, Harrison nodded marginally.

"But what I *didn't* see and do not see now is guilt."

Harrison's eyes welled with tears. "Thank you, sir."

"Please. Don't call me sir. Makes me feel older than what I am," he said with a soft smile.

"Sorry. Thank you, Michael."

"There's also the fact that the girl didn't point a finger at you right away at the lineup. She hesitated, which indicates to me that she wasn't absolutely certain it was you."

"Yeah. She did hesitate. It blew me over when she suddenly said it was me. I knew I didn't do it…I had been arrested for driving under the influence…My first time, by the way. I assure you, if I ever do get out of here, it won't happen again. But how did you know about that? Her hesitation?"

"It's all right here in the documents." Michael gave his briefcase a pat.

"So they do keep note of everything?"

"They do. After all, folk's lives depend on it."

"That's for sure."

"And I had every intention of coming in yesterday evening, but I got a call on another case just as I was heading out the door to come here and had to focus my attentions there."

"Well, again, thank you."

"Tell you what. Save the thanks for when you're found innocent."

Harrison nodded.

"Well." Michael stood, taking up his briefcase. "Mona or I will be seeing you soon."

"I'm indebted to you."

With a wave of his hand, Michael signaled to the guard that he was ready, and the guard let him out. As he walked out of the county jail door and skipped down the concrete steps he tried to discern what it was about Rick Harrison that just wouldn't go away. He opened the door to his black BMW and tossed in his briefcase to the passenger side, slipped in behind the steering wheel and stared into the rearview mirror at the gray eyes – Eyes! That was it! Rick Harrison's eyes were the same hazel hue that Darren's were. They were even similar in shape. "What do you know," he muttered to himself. Rick Harrison bears a slight resemblance to that sometimes insufferable son of mine."

The sun was out much too bright for Gavril to dare step out. Even though he had fed well the evening before, he thirsted again – something that never really ended – but quenching it would have to wait. In the meantime, he would just sip on the wine he had stashed in the refrigerator. Fortunately for vampires, it took a lot of alcohol to make one drunk, and it was excellent for staving off the often maddening blood hunger. He downed a couple of gulps from a small glass he kept in the pocket of his blazer for such occasions, as not all apartments and hotels had shot glasses available. Of course, he could use regular glasses, but he preferred his own. This one he had kept for over a hundred years. It had been given to him by Elsa, a German girl that he had hoped to turn, but unfortunately, he had ended up killing her when she caught him feeding from one of her female friends in an alley. Not something he had desired or planned to do, but her screams had brought the attention of the denizens in the streets, and he had killed her instantly to quiet her, and then vanished with her in his arms, burying her later in an old cemetery just outside of Berlin. There, he told her he was sorry and wished that things had been different. He knew she couldn't hear, but hoped that, somehow, she would know that he did love her and never wanted to kill her; had wanted to spend eternity with her. However, that had not happened. The memory still often haunted him. He didn't want something like that to ever happen again.

Mona was surprised to see Darren sitting behind Michael's desk, rummaging through the drawers, when she walked in. He sat forward with a start, apparently not expecting her so soon. He glanced at his watch. "Oh! I guess it is eight."

Even though Darren was Michael's son, she couldn't help the thread of suspicion tugging at her gut. What was he going through Michael's things for?

It was as though she had thought out loud. "I was just looking for Dad's extra key to the storage room in the basement. I seem to have lost mine."

"Oh! Well, I have Michael's," she responded, sitting down her purse and digging the key out for him. She handed it over. "Just make sure you don't forget to return it. I had to get some files for him earlier. That's why it wasn't in his desk."

"In the basement?"

It was rare that they went to the basement, and for them both to need something there did seem a bit odd. "Yes."

A peculiar expression stole over his face. "Mind telling me what file you needed?"

"I'm not sure I should say, Darren. Michael doesn't want anyone to know at this time."

"Come on, Mona! I'm his son. You can trust me."

She sniggered at the latter. "Oh…really?"

"You know what I mean, dammit."

"All right. But I have to tell Michael I told you."

"Fine by me."

"He wanted the file on Tim Brown."

Something in Darren's eyes flickered. He cleared his throat. "Tim Brown?"

"Yes. Why?"

"Never mind. I guess it's not that important." He didn't want her to know that it was the file he was after.

"You're sure?"

"Yes!" he replied, turning pallid. "Think I drank too much last night."

"You okay, Darren? You don't look so good."

"Actually, I am a little sick to my stomach." He handed the key back to her. "I don't need this right now." He hurried on out the door.

"That was just a little weird," she said to herself.

It was only a few minutes after five when it clouded over and began to rain. Gavril was not unhappy about that. He could go outside now. Even if it stopped raining, according to the weatherman on the television, it wasn't going to clear up until tomorrow.

He slipped into jeans and a red Tee shirt. Even dressed casually, he still had an air of sophistication about him that simply would not go unnoticed. Still turned heads in a crowd. He could vanish at will, though, and often did when his presence seemed to draw more attention than desired.

He slipped quietly down the stairs and into the drugstore, where Harry greeted him with a broad smile and asked if the apartment was okay, and did he need anything. Gavril replied that it was just fine; that it would do for now, until he knew whether he wanted to remain in Seattle or not.

Once outside in the cool misting rain, Gavril began his search for just the right person to satiate his hunger. An elderly man with a cane limped by, eyeing him warily. Perhaps he sensed something. Sometimes the older ones had more of a keen sense of danger, having been around longer. No. He wouldn't do.

Sometimes the blood of the elderly had a bit of a bitter aftertaste that tended to linger. It wasn't always the case, but he had had enough of the unpleasant aftertaste enough times to warrant him leaving the aged alone. It had been his experience that the younger the meal the better. Only he drew the line at children. He would not harm a child and would quickly eliminate anyone whom he thought guilty of doing so.

As he watched the throng of people pass to and fro, his thoughts turned to Mona; simply thinking about her brought certain warmth to his genitals. His desire for her was growing faster than he cared to admit. He did his best to push her from his thoughts. She looked so much like Alina. It was uncanny. He needed to focus on feeding. Otherwise, he might lose control if she came in his presence, for his desire to mate and feed from her could quickly become overwhelming. That he did not want to happen.

A couple of attractive young ladies, he guessed to be between twenty and twenty-five, at the corner newsstand caught his attention with their light laughter. The redhead with a pony tail and face sprinkled with light freckles was eyeing him flirtatiously, and the brunette had her back to him, but kept glancing over her shoulder in his direction. He could hear every word they said. They were commenting on how hot he was for an older man and wondered if he was good in bed.

His smile was wickedly buoyant. He had found his meal.

He approached them, introduced himself, chatting charmingly for a few minutes, and then offered to buy them dinner. The girls shared big grins, unable to suppress their pleasant surprise and simultaneously replied yes.

"Good!" he said, taking each by an arm and leading them down to a small sidewalk café, where he kept his promise to feed them.

The girls laughed at basically everything it seemed, flirting with him to the point of bordering on the outrageous. He was more than aware that he could be irresistible when he so desired, but these young ladies were asking for it. They obviously wanted to get laid. What's more, being the vampire he was, he was willing to oblige, for the hunger for blood went hand in hand with sexual desire.

When they finished their burgers and fries, he let them lead the way to the redhead's Volvo, which was parked on a side street. The windows were tinted and no one could see in, perfect for some private time together. There, he made love to the redhead first, and then he took his turn with the brunette. Both were so overwhelmed by his passionate embrace that they wanted more. He sat back, eyeing them in his most attractive but wicked way and asked. "You sure you want more?"

"Oh yes!" the brunette breathed hotly. "Yes!"

With an eyebrow raised, he regarded the redhead. She bobbed her head yes very enthusiastically.

"Guess I must oblige then." He made love to them again, and then put them under his spell and drank from both, leaving them alive but very anemic and unconscious in the car. He vanished then and returned to his apartment. Eventually they would awaken and realize something had happened to them, but would not know what. He wasn't too concerned about it. After all, he was a vampire, and he could have just as easily killed them both, but they were young and had been very generous in their affections, so he decided to let them live.

Chapter Three:

It was a pleasant surprise for Mona when Michael invited her to dinner that evening. She realized that it must have been written all over her face, for he confessed that he knew he was a little old for her, by about thirty years, but he admitted that his interest in her was more than the fact that she was a damn good secretary; admitted that he was and had been attracted to her for some time, but because of his being so much older, and of her relationship with Darren, he had kept a respectable distance. Now, he figured there would be no harm in their sharing a meal together.

She placed her white cloth napkin on her lap and smiled pleasantly over at Michael, who sat across the table from her, looking hopeful. "I have to admit, Michael, that you are an interesting man. You really don't look a day over forty-five, but I happen to know you're a little older than that."

"Nearing fifty-one, Mona. I keep in shape, though."

"I know. You're been working out three times a week, ever since I've been working for the firm."

"And I put in half a day every Saturday morning. Have for the past twenty years or so." An amused grin appeared at the corners of his mouth.

"What?"

"Darren...I know he's young and healthy now, but he doesn't take as good of care of himself as I. He claims to work out twice a week, but I happen to know that he misses more often than not."

"You're right about that."

"He just may regret it when he's my age, if he doesn't start taking better care of himself now."

"I wouldn't doubt it."

The waiter came and refilled their wine glasses. Michael smiled cordially and thanked him. He turned his attention back to Mona and the waiter disappeared among the tables. "I want to thank you for having dinner with me this evening. It means a lot to this aging fella."

"Don't put yourself down, Michael. You're still very attractive." She meant it. He was good-looking. What's more, she was also pretty sure that in the shape he was in, he was probably very good in bed. She was surprised that she had such a thought and experienced an instant warm surge to her cheeks.

Michael noticed and cocked his head. "Did I say something to embarrass you?"

She bit her bottom lip, attempting to contain her grin, and shyly glanced down. "Nothing you said. Just something that crossed my mind."

He apparently had a good idea of what she was thinking and reflected her grin when she looked back up. "Okay, Mona. Let's just enjoy these rib-eyes." He winked and began carving his steak, smiling sagaciously every now and then.

Nancy looked up from her Kindle, eyes focused on Darren, who hadn't stopped pacing for the last half hour. "For God's sake, Darren. What is wrong with you?"

Darren stopped midstride. "I'm sorry, Nancy. I have a lot on my mind."

Nancy twisted her mouth around and laid her Kindle on the coffee table. "Okay. Out with it."

"With what?"

"Dah! Whatever in hell is causing you to wear a path into the damn living room carpet?"

"Huh?" He glanced down at the floor. Sure enough, the rug threads were actually flattened where he'd been treading back and forth. He laughed nervously. "You're right." He offered her a fake smile, dropped down beside her and loosened his tie. "Okay. I did something really stupid a while back. Something I shouldn't have done. And I'm afraid my dad's going to find out."

Eyeing him abruptly, she asked, "What in hell did you do, Darren? I know you've always been competitive with your father, but it never once occurred to me that you would do anything to cross him."

"I didn't cross him…exactly."

"Okay…" This was a side of Darren she'd never seen before. "Then what *did* you do?"

He sniffed and then swiped the back of his hand across his nostrils before dropping his hand down. "You know me, Nancy. I may not be exactly the nicest guy in the world, but, normally, I am pretty much on the up and up."

Chewing her mouth around, she responded, "Uh-huh."

His hands went to his face and he began crying, bent over, elbows resting on his knees. "I did something really terrible, Nancy."

"…How terrible, Darren?"

He blew out air and sat back, wiping his eyes with a white handkerchief that he took from his vest pocket, and said, "I don't want to lose you, Nancy."

Her eyes softened. "What did you do that makes you think you would lose me?"

He knew how to play her. She was self-centered and needed to be important, needed to be number one. He was also aware that she wanted to be at the top, wanted to be with the man that would run the law firm one day – And that should be him. "Do you remember the Tim Brown case?"

She thought about it a minute. "Sounds familiar…What about it?"

"I was doing the legwork for Dad at the time. Was just fresh out of law school. Dad had me running everywhere. Anyway, he acquired this moment of conscience, I guess. Whatever one might call it, and thought he might want to defend the man. Most of the time we work for those who can afford us, but once in a while he gets it in his head that he needs to defend someone he believes might be innocent but doesn't have any money. Someone who can't afford a top lawyer. To get to the point, I may have lied to my dad about some of the facts in the case."

"What? Why on earth would you do that?"

He shrugged. "Not sure why now," he lied. "Maybe I thought it would hurt our image. Was pretty certain he was guilty. Thought Dad was nuts. Didn't want him to defend him. Anyway, there are some similarities in the Rick Harrison case. It set me to thinking that they might possibly be connected." Another lie, for he knew the truth. "So, I tried to get the file, but it was no longer available. Mona told me that Dad has it."

"Someone from the firm must have represented this Tim Brown. Otherwise, why would the file be in the firm's basement?"

"No one with us represented him. However, Dad had me put together what I had on the man and file it away. That's why the file was there. I have wanted to get rid of it for a long time, but I was afraid to, in case my dad ever did want it. How could I explain to him that I had thrown it away?"

"After all this time, and the firm didn't even represent the man, I would have thought that the file would have been done away with by now."

Darren sniggered. "You really don't know my dad, do you?"

"I'm sure I don't know him as well as you."

"He *never* throws out a file. Says one never knows when something might come up that would be needed in one of them."

Nancy half smiled. "Maybe that is one of the reasons your father is such a good lawyer."

"Maybe so. But that's not helping me now. Dad has the file."

"And you're afraid he's going to find out you weren't completely honest with him?"

"Yes. Knowing my father, I am sure he will realize it."

Her lips parted in a reassuring smile and her deep dimples showed markedly. "I think you are worrying too much about it, Darren. Even if he realizes there are things in the file that don't quite click, the man was still found guilty. I have doubts that it will matter now."

Darren bobbed his head and sighed reflectively. "You're right. I am, perhaps, worrying far too much about it." He stood and shifted up his slacks. "Let's go have dinner somewhere. How about Olive Garden again?"

"Sound's scrumptious to me. Let me get my purse."

He watched her walk off down the short hall to their bedroom; her tall slender body slightly swaying ever so attractively. He considered that she should have been a model, instead of a legal secretary. He hoped she was right. Maybe he was worrying too much. Still, his father was damn good at what he did. If he looked hard enough, long enough, some things might just begin to click. Things he didn't want his father to put together, like similarities in builds and eye color, to name a few.

Gavril was home by ten p.m., believing Mona would be in by then, but he knew the instant he stepped into their hall that she wasn't. Her lovely scent lingered, but it wasn't fresh, wasn't as wonderful as when she was there. "Oh well," he said under his breath and let himself into his apartment. He had all the time in the world. Waiting was something he was very good at. He poured himself a shot of whiskey and sat down in an old leather recliner that had definitely seen better days, but it was clean. That sufficed for him. After all, this wasn't a permanent home.

Mona knew she'd drank a little more wine than what she was used to, but Michael was such good company – knew just the right things to say to a woman – that she forgot about the time. That is, until he checked his watch and apologized for keeping her out so late. They both needed to get going. He had an early case in court, and needed her there with him.

Gavril sat the recliner forward the second he heard Mona's musical laughter on the sidewalk below. She wasn't alone. There was a more mature gentleman with her, a man she was referring to as Michael. Had to be Mona's ex-boyfriend's father. Gavril knew this from little bits of pieces of conversations he had had with Harry Butler. Harry felt a certain fatherly responsibility towards Mona, as she no longer had her own. Harry wasn't sure if the man was dead or just not around, but he knew Mona said she hadn't seen him since she was nine. Her mother, Gloria Sims, lived across the Puget Sound in Bremerton.

Gavril stepped back from the window and poured himself another shot of whiskey and then took a unit of blood from the refrigerator. He would take turns sipping on them. He had hoped to sample the sweetness of Mona's blood this evening, but he knew now that it probably wasn't going to happen. He could force himself on her, and hypnotize her to forget, but that wasn't what he wanted at all. No. It wasn't his style when wishing to court a desirable, potential mate. He sat back in the recliner once more, listening intently, as Mona and Michael stepped up to her door. Apparently Michael was good company; for this was the most Gavril had heard her laugh since he'd first laid eyes on her. He could also tell by the timbre of Michael's voice that he was very much enjoying Mona's company, as well. This was not good news. There was a strong possibility that Mona would lean towards the older, more distinguished and attractive man after being jilted by his son. What's more, it was more than apparent to Gavril that that was what the older gentleman was hoping for. He titled his head back and tossed the rest of his drink to the back of his throat, swallowed, and sat his glass and unit of blood down. No. This was not good at all.

He stood.

Mona asked Michael if he wanted to come in for bit. There was a moment of obvious, stunned silence. Apparently Michael had not anticipated Mona's coming around to him so quickly. His voice cracked briefly as he stated that he'd love to, but it was late and they did have to be in court early.

"All right," her sweet voice replied.

"I'll take a rain check, though," Michael said with a subtle smile.

There was another moment of silence – Gavril sensed a hug -- and then Mona opened her door and went inside, and Michael's footfalls could be heard exiting down the hall.

Gavril was relieved. He really didn't desire to kill the older Graves. There was a certain decency about him. Unfortunately,

Gavril couldn't say that for the son. Still, he had it in his heart to have Mona for his mate. It was good that the older Graves had left. Now, he would have to move a little faster than he had anticipated in order to heighten Mona's interest in him. Until now, he had taken his time, not previously foreseeing the older Graves as possible competition.

Mona was a little surprised by the mixed feelings she was experiencing. She'd always thought Michael handsome, but he was old enough to be her father. The thought of them having any kind of personal relationship had never occurred to her, until now. "Oh this is silly," she mumbled to herself as she went off to shower and ready for bed.

Still, by the time she slipped under the covers Michael's handsome face was still very much in her mind's eye. She was tired and didn't dwell on it too long, falling asleep within just a few minutes.

Only she didn't dream about Michael.

It was evening and she stood in the middle of an ornate garden, had a New Orleans essence. At least, she thought it was a garden, until she noticed something that appeared to be a tall headstone off to her right. "Huh?" There was a low-lying fog. She glanced down. It covered her feet. The dream was so real, so vivid; she believed she was actually there. "What am I doing here?"

Silence. Dark, dank silence. A barely detectable mist tickled her cheeks.

Off in the distance, on a high hill above the fog, to her right, she noticed a magnificent old structure – a castle! "What the—?" She did a three-hundred-and-sixty-degree turn, scanning her surroundings thoroughly. Where was she? She slowly took a step forward and then another. More headstones came into view as the fog parted slightly as though to allow her passage. "Where am I?" There was a fluttering of wings, and a large black bird, a raven, flew off to her left. Something innate knew she was dreaming, but it was all so incredibly clear that she was beyond alarmed. "Why am I in a freakin' cemetery?" Then looking back at the ancient castle, she said, "And what country am I in?" There was a heavy, foreboding feel to it all. She wanted to wake up, but for some reason she remained a prisoner of her dream. Now she was truly frightened; afraid she was trapped in a dream that was quickly becoming a nightmare.

"Oh God!" she cried aloud. "Why can't I wake up?" Suddenly the fog parted right in front of her, revealing a headstone that she had not noticed before. Across the face of it was written Mona Sims. She screamed and bolted upright in bed, gasping. *"Oh God! Oh God!"*

There was a light but audible knock at her apartment door. "Mona? Mona, are you all right?"

She recognized the soft but crystal clear voice of her new neighbor, Gavril Conta.

"Mona?" He called again.

It took a moment for the vivid dream to fade and for her thoughts to clear enough for her function. She grabbed her robe off the foot of her bed, quickly slipped into it and made her way to the door which she opened only slightly.

Captivating black eyes peered in at her, seemingly full of concern. "I heard you scream. Are you okay?"

Embarrassed now, she quickly replied, "I had…a stupid nightmare. I'm sorry. I didn't mean to wake anyone."

His reply was kind and understanding. "No need for apology, Mona. I just wanted to make sure you were okay. I feared that someone had broken in and that you were in trouble."

Just then, Harry rushed out of his room, wearing a gray, terrycloth bathrobe and gray slippers to match, and headed their way to see what was going on.

Gavril turned to him just as he approached. "It seems the little lady had a nightmare," he articulately explained.

Harry briefly glanced at her in relief. "Whew! I was afraid one of those thugs off the street had finally managed to pick one of the locks." He smiled comfortingly then. "I'm just glad you're okay, Mona. Now Matilda and I can go back to sleep." He glanced down the hall where his wife had her head full of pink curlers stuck out the door. She waved.

Mona waved back. "I'm sorry! Jeeze! I didn't mean to wake up the entire building. Didn't mean to wake anyone up."

Harry gestured with a flip of his hand. "No need for apologies, Mona. Just do your best to go back to sleep. Hopefully, this time without any nightmares."

Eyeing her obscurely and almost appearing a little amused, Gavril agreed, "Yes. Get some rest."

There was something in Gavril's stare, which she found mystifying and a bit creepy at the same time. She couldn't pinpoint it exactly, but it did get her attention. As before, she found his presence profoundly intriguing. She almost forgot about her nightmare.

Harry broke the moment by saying, "Well, I hope you sleep well the rest of the night." He disappeared into his apartment with Matilda.

"…Yes. Thank you. I'll try," she replied, looking off in Harry's direction.

Gavril gently touched Mona's shoulder. "I, too, hope you'll sleep well."

As she turned back to face Gavril, she noticed an ornate, gold ring on his forefinger. It held what appeared to be a huge ruby. "That's some ring you have there."

A pleased smile crossed his full lips. "It's a family heirloom. Been in my family for hundreds of years. In fact, I am not even sure how old it is."

"Whoa!"

"Glad you find it interesting," he said, smiling, those black depths holding her prisoner with their paralyzing gaze.

"It's beautiful!"

He winked. "You get some rest now, young lady." An eyebrow hiked. "Perhaps I'll see you tomorrow?"

"Perhaps."

He turned, moving with incredible silence, and went back to his apartment.

Somewhat confused, she closed her door. Now, Gavril was all she could think about. And that scent! What was it? Pine and sage mixed with something else? Whatever it was, it was captivating. Lingering. Then, out of nowhere, she envisioned herself naked and in Gavril's arms, being ravished by him. What's more, she wasn't just enjoying it – She loved it! At once, she was all hot and bothered, wanted him to make love to her. "Oh shit!" she said to herself, realizing this stranger was not in any sense *ordinary*. He seemed to have some kind of power over her. Still, he was, for all outward appearances, very refined, sophisticated, and probably came from a family of great wealth. So what was he doing living in a low-income apartment over a drugstore in Seattle?

No sooner had Darren sat down to his desk and his dad came in the room. "Dad! You're here! I thought you'd be in court?"

"We had a case scheduled, but Judge Maker had some kind of emergency. His wife was in an accident or something. No other judges free at the moment. Anyway, they put the hearing off until next week."

"Oh…well." Darren shuffled some papers around on his desk, as though he were busy.

"Mona told me you were looking for the Tim Brown file." He peered out the window. One could see the Space Needle in the distance. "Any particular reason?"

Darren cleared his throat. His dad was not easily fooled. He decided that at this moment, some honesty would be the wisest approach. "Yes! I believe there are some similarities in the Harrison case. Thought I'd check it out for you."

"Unusually thoughtful of you, son." Michael turned back eyeing him curiously.

"Simply trying to be helpful."

His dad's expression revealed that he wasn't totally buying it, but he was willing to give it the benefit of a doubt. "All right. Appreciate it. But I believe Mona and I have it covered. Besides, I know you have several cases right now…Enough to keep you busy." He turned to walk out.

"You're right, Dad. I do."

Michael stopped at the door and looked back at his son. "Would it bother you if I were to ask Mona out?"

Darren's face went through a gamut of expressions before he finally said, "What?"

"You heard me. You know I've always liked Mona, but I figured that even though you've always been somewhat a jerk with the ladies, that she was your girl. Only, now you're with Nancy. I had dinner with Mona last night. We had fun. I want to ask her out again. Of course I can without your blessings, but just thought I would ask…since you are my son. You wouldn't have a problem with it, would you?"

Though Darren was uncomfortable with his father seeing Mona, he knew he had no right to be. After all, he had left her for Nancy, something he was beginning to regret but wasn't willing to openly admit yet. He surmised his father suspected as such. That bugged him. His father was the last person he wanted to admit to that he had screwed up royally. "Sure, Dad. You have my blessings."

"Good! I was hoping you'd see it that way." With a brisk turn, he walked out.

"Dammit!" Darren picked up a pencil, angrily snapping it in half and hurled it across the room.

Mona was glad their court appointment had been put off. She was still shaken from the previous night's nightmare. She had fallen back to sleep, but had not slept nearly as well as she would have liked. More dreams had come to haunt her, although not quite as disconcerting as the one in the cemetery. First, she'd had a dream about Darren and Michael. They were arguing over her and she had been trying to break them up, begging them to stop. Paying her no heed, they came to blows. She screamed and screamed, but it was as though she wasn't even there. They didn't seem to hear her at all. She dropped down to her knees, crying bitterly, and then suddenly Gavril was there, offering out a hand, telling her everything would be all right. He assisted her in standing and wrapped a gentle arm around her waist. "Come on," he said, as she stared at the men who were still battling it out, "let me take you someplace quiet." He gestured with an outstretched arm. "Someplace away from all this."

She bobbed her head in submission, not knowing what to expect. In a wisp of a moment, she stood in front of the majestic gray castle she'd seen in her previous dream. Only now, it grandly loomed before them. Gavril was at her side, and she leaned into him, clutching his arm. They stood on a grand walkway shrouded by tall trees and floral gardens that led to the large double front doors. There was a loud clap of thunder, and lightning streaked menacingly across the darkening sky. Yet, it failed to alarm her. With his free arm, Gavril gestured towards the door, indicating that they should go inside. She marveled at the prospect of seeing what was inside. Yet, she marveled even more at her handsome escort, who simply took her breath away just gazing upon him. Then she awoke, sitting up in bed and it was breaking dawn.

It had been too early to dress for work, so she opted to take a long, warm shower to soothe her frayed nerves. She stayed under the spray until the water began to run cold. At which time, she shut it off, stepped out and toweled off and dressed. She had stayed in the shower longer than she realized and had to pick up her pace, hurrying out the door.

Gavril had been just outside his apartment door, had a Styrofoam cup of steaming coffee in his hand – she surmised he'd gone downstairs where coffee was kept going all day in the back of the drugstore. Wearing that vague, strange smile of his, he had bid her good morning and went on into his apartment. Though it appeared innocent enough, she had a spooky feeling that he had been waiting for her to come out. Only why would he do that? The coffee *was* hot. She decided she was just imagining things. Blamed it on her weird dreams that he seemed to have a prominent roll in.

Mona barely had time to place her purse in a side drawer of her desk when Michael called her into his office. She snatched up a pad and pen and hurried in.

"No need to take notes. I didn't call you in for that."

"Oh?"

Her expression of surprise made him smile. "I want you to know I had a wonderful time last night."

"I enjoyed it too."

"Enjoyed?" he asked, eyes probing for a more in-depth response. "I didn't say I enjoyed it. I said I had a *wonderful* time. I don't know about you, but to me wonderful carries a little more weight than enjoyed."

"Oh! I'm sorry. I didn't mean—."

He chuckled. "I'm giving you a hard time, Mona. Relax."

She shrugged. "I admit…You have me a bit flustered. Not sure what you're getting at."

"Aren't you? Think about it." His eyes searched hers. "I know I'm old enough to be your father, but I've always found you very attractive. What's more, I am sure you are aware that Margaret and I are married in name only. She has her…Shall we say, other interests. We stayed together for years because of Darren and Richard. Of course, both are grown now. These last few years, we've stayed together more for social reasons. She loves the social life. As far as her friends know, we have a great marriage. And I let her have her little charade."

"I know it's none of my business, but you said she has other interests. Are you saying she hasn't been completely faithful?"

"She's had an affair or two. In fact, she's seeing someone now. And I won't lie. Had one myself about five years ago, but I didn't really love the woman. She didn't love me either. She just wanted to give her husband payback for having been unfaithful to her. I'm a man. Margaret and I don't sleep together anymore. I enjoyed the benefits." He smiled with a little twist of his mouth.

Having a good idea where he might be going with this, she asked, "Are you saying you want to have an affair with me?" She sat down in a corner chair. In the back of her mind, she feared that she might, in the future, lose her job if things didn't work out between her and Michael. "I…"

"I really prefer not to label it as an affair. I value our relationship more than that. You do find me attractive, don't you? Or am I getting so old that I can't truly read the signs anymore?"

"You're not old, Michael. And to answer your first question – I do find you attractive. It's just that I have apprehensions. You are my boss. Not just my boss—." She was going to say that he was the head of the law firm.

He held up a hand, stopping her. "You won't lose your job, if things don't work out between us, Mona. You can rest at ease. I would never do that to you. I'm not Darren." He titled his head slightly forward in emphasis.

"I know you're not. I've often wished Darren was more like you."

He stood and came around from behind his desk, reaching for her hand and had her stand. He studied her face. "You are so beautiful. Darren is such a fool. Don't make me beg, Mona. Please have dinner with me again. Give me a chance to show you that we can be good together. What do you say?"

Turning her eyes up to his, she replied. "Maybe you're right. I see no harm in giving it…as you say…a try."

He grinned the biggest grin she'd ever seen on him. "Tonight? Olive Garden? And after that," he said, still smiling, "we'll decide where to go from there."

She reflected his smile.

He pulled her close and kissed her for the first time. He was a good kisser, surprisingly better than Darren. She responded more enthusiastically than she would have anticipated.

"Whoa…" he said, breaking the kiss and pulling back from her a little. "I hope I can concentrate on my clients the rest of the day."

She smiled with her eyes.

"I hate to change the subject now… But would you please get that Hampton fella, who has left a ton of messages, since yesterday, on the phone for me? Not sure I want to take his case… But maybe someone else in the firm would be willing to take him on. Possibly Darren?" He grinned mischievously.

There was laughter in her eyes. "You got it."

He winked and she went back to her office to get Hampton on the line.

It was noon when Mona ran into Nancy at the watercooler. Nancy gave Mona a disdainful sneer as she drank down her water, wrinkled the tiny paper cup in her hands and let it drop contemptuously into the wastebasket. Mona just stared back, unmoving and unmoved. It was all too apparent that Nancy considered herself in a secure place now, being Darren's girlfriend. Mona smiled politely and headed for the elevator, as she had some errands to run for Michael before going to lunch. Wouldn't Nancy just flip if she knew that poor little Mona was dating the head honcho of Graves & Son. That thought made her feel on top of the world and it showed in her step when she practically danced into the elevator.

"Going down," she told the handsome Hispanic youth, Roberto, who ran the elevator. His sparkling black eyes at once reminded her of Gavril's. Only they weren't as intense and mysterious.

"Down it is, Miss Sims."

Rick Harrison shoved his tray aside and ran long fingers through his hair, before dropping them down to his sides. How could he eat? He had been accused of raping a young girl! The only thing he was guilty of was drinking too much and driving. Even in a state of alcoholic stupor, he didn't rape anyone, especially a young girl. That much, he was certain. Why she had accused him, though, was beyond his comprehension. He was still trying to wrap his mind around it. Why? Why did she accuse him? He loved his own teenage daughters – Lisa, Ann and Marie – more than anything in the world. He would gladly lay down his life for them, and he would want to kill anyone who would try to harm them. There was no way he could hurt another man's daughter. Hell no!

The guard on duty appeared and told him he had a visitor, unlocked the gate and slid it open. Rick wondered if it was that lawyer, Michael Graves. He followed the officer down the hall and was led to the room where Michael Graves was waiting. The lawyer smiled and told him to take a chair, which he did.

"I just want to go over the night of the alleged rape," Michael said.

Rick snickered cynically. "Afraid I can't help you much there. I got soused off my ass. Guess I was driving all over the road when the cops caught up with me."

"Yes. That's all here. However, I want to go over the hours before. Why did you get drunk in the first place?"

"Judy… That's my wife. Soon to be ex, from what she's told me. Anyway, Judy had just informed me she was leaving me. We had a bad argument. The girls were crying. So, I left."

"You mean your daughters?"

"Yes. Lisa, Ann and Marie… And no. We didn't name them after any Presleys. My oldest sister is named Lisa. My wife's mother, Ann. And my grandmother on my father's side was Marie. Guess we weren't very imaginative when we named our kids, so we just gave them family names."

"Nothing wrong with that," Michael stated.

"Believe me… We have regretted it at times. Folks can't seem to keep from connecting their names with the Presleys, somehow."

"I can see where that might be a problem." Michael gave an understanding nod. He opened up his briefcase and took out a pad and pen. He could record everything on his iPhone, but he preferred to write things down. "Now, I know you've been over this a hundred times in the past, but I want you to go over it with me now. I want you to tell me every little detail about the night you were brought in and charged with the rape of the Gilbert girl."

"Okay. Not sure it will do any good. But if that's what you need?"

"It is." Michael clicked his pen open. "Start from the very beginning."

Darren stood at the door to his office hoping to catch Mona as she left work. He'd sent Nancy downstairs to look for some files on an old case. He really didn't need them. He just wanted a chance to talk to Mona before she left. He glanced at his watch. It had been ten minutes since he sent Nancy downstairs. She'd be back soon. "Come on, Mona!" he said under his breath, smiling nervously at one of the other secretaries walking by on her way out, eyeing him curiously. Just then, he heard Mona's light, musical laughter and she appeared out of his dad's office with his dad. "Dammit!" he hissed. He hadn't realized his dad had come back, thought he was still at the county jail.

Michael noticed him before Mona did, and it was apparent to Darren that his dad knew exactly what he was waiting for, from his cat-like grin. "Haven't left yet, Darren?"

"No," he said, now eyeing Nancy who'd just stepped out of the elevator into the hall and was heading their way with the files he'd sent for in her hands. "Just waiting for Nancy. Sent her after some files I needed."

"Well, don't work too hard. Mona and I are going to dinner at Olive Garden." He eyed Nancy who'd just approached them. "You two want to join us?"

Nancy swiveled her head around, giving Darren a curiously confused stare.

"No. That's okay, Dad. Nancy and I have other plans."

"We do?" Nancy asked.

"Yes…Yea…You forgot that we're going to the Outback for steaks."

Still puzzled, she replied, "Oh! I guess I did."

Reading them both like a book, Michael smiled complacently and said, "Well, you two enjoy your steaks. Maybe some other time?"

Mona bid them a good evening and went with Michael to the elevator.

Nancy turned to Darren. "Just what in hell was that about?"

"An invitation to dinner. Why?"

Her brow narrowed. She didn't believe him. "Your dad's dating Mona now, isn't he?"

He did his best to be nonchalant. "Hey…I broke up with her. She can see whomever she wants."

"Your dad's married."

"So. You think my mother would really care?"

She thought about it a minute. "No."

"Then don't worry about it."

"I don't remember anything about eating at Outback."

"I lied, Nancy. Get over it."

Her mouth gaped, incredulous. So we're *not* going to dinner?"

"We can go eat steaks. I don't care. It's just that my dad seems to think he's getting to me by dating Mona."

She snorted. "Looks like it's working."

"On the contrary," he flashed a smile and hung an arm around her shoulder, "that is just not so. I don't care about Mona. I have you. My dad's attitude is what is pissing me off… Let's toss those files on my desk… They can wait until tomorrow. And let's go get those steaks."

Her face relaxed. Still, the lack of complete trust was in her eyes.

Neither Mona nor Michael noticed the dark stranger pursuing them, keeping back in the shadows out of sight. Nor did they notice him as he entered the restaurant and take a small table on the far side of the establishment. Even though he was a good distance from them, he could hear every word spoken, for his hearing was sharper than any dog's. Over the years, he had learned to tune out the extra noises and focus on just what he wanted or needed to hear.

It was obvious that Mona enjoyed the older man's companionship. He was gentlemanly enough, gracious and attentive. Gavril surmised him to be the total opposite of Darren, who was much more self-centered and immature, in spite of his education and background. And wasn't that the way it often happened? A child born with the proverbial silver spoon in their mouth often did not appreciate or understand how lucky they were; often ruining their own lives, in spite of all the gifts and advantages that life had bestowed upon them. Yes. Gavril could see it quite clearly. Darren was no exception.

Gavril almost felt sorry for Michael, whom he could see had achieved his status with hard work and study. He was a man who did understand the values of what he had and appreciated them. He was a man who wanted the best for his son, but also knew that his son did not deserve it. Also, Gavril could clearly see that the man was more than interested in Mona. This, Gavril did not like. He considered Mona his. Still, he had some reservations about harming a good man. There had been a time, when he was first turned, that it would have been of little concern to him, but through the long years of seeing so much pain and suffering, he had come to appreciate a good soul when he saw one. Michael Graves was a good soul. No. This was going to take extra work.

He could easily put Mona under his spell and render her subject to his every whim and desire. Only that was not what he wanted. For to be whole, he desired a mate that chose to be with him, not one that was compelled to do so. That was something he could do anytime with any woman he wished, but it wouldn't mean anything to him on a personal basis. He'd already had countless women under those circumstances. Most of them, he couldn't even remember their names.

When the waiter came, Gavril ordered spaghetti and meatballs with a salad. Although there was a partial partition between him and the far side of the restaurant, decorated with bulbous white vases of splaying vines, he could still observe the couple of interest through a space between two of the vases. The couple took their time eating, which gave Gavril more than sufficient time to consume his meal. When the waiter returned and inquired as to whether he wanted desert, he ordered a slice of apple pie. He was doing his best to time his stay with the couple's. Sure enough, just as he finished his pie, the couple's waiter approached with their bill. Gavril summoned for his.

After paying for his meal, he waited for a minute, anticipating Michael and Mona to do the same. He stood when they did, approaching the foyer at approximately the same instant. Here he feigned great surprise at their meeting. "How pleasant seeing you here, Mona," he said, smiling cordially; eyes flickering with little lights as they turned to her escort, who was scrutinizing him closely.

"Oh! Hi, Gavril!" Mona's response was a little delayed at the surprise of seeing Gavril there. She turned to Michael. "Michael, this is my new neighbor, Count Gavril Conta... I think." She tilted her head around to Gavril. "That is right, isn't it?"

"Correct," he replied, regarding Michael just as closely as he was being scrutinized.

"And this is Michael Graves."

Michael's expression was dubious as he reached out to shake Gavril's hand. "A Count, huh?"

"Again, correct," Gavril responded with a quirk on his lips. He released Michael's hand.

"Mind if I ask where you are from?"

"Not at all. Romania," Gavril replied with a secret behind his smile. "You know. Dracula's home."

"Ah yes... Dracula, the legendary vampire. But then... He really wasn't a vampire, was he?" Michael was still ambivalent of Gavril.

"No. But he was still a monster in his own right." Gavril didn't mind Michael's suspiciousness. The man wasn't wet behind the ears. It was distrustful, in true instinctive, protective mode. That was okay with Gavril. The man was looking out for the lady. He would have less respect for the man if he saw otherwise.

"Well," Michael said, easing an arm around Mona's waist, "nice meeting you. We will probably meet again, since you are Mona's neighbor."

"No doubt. Nice meeting you too." He gave a slight curtsey, holding out an arm for them to go out the door first. Outside, they went to the right, and he went to the left. They did not know he wasn't in a car. It didn't matter. Soon as they were gone, he walked behind the building and disappeared.

Chapter Four:

Darren did his best to focus on Nancy sitting before him. He did love the beautiful golden shine of her brown hair that was almost red, but not quite, and those limpid brown eyes. She was tall, too, almost as tall as he. He was six foot. He considered that if only her personality had matched her physical beauty, she would be a real keeper. They had finished their meal and moved on to her favorite nightclub for a few drinks and dancing. It really wasn't something he wanted to do, but he knew he had to, somehow, convince her that things were good with them. The last thing he needed right now was the fury of her wrath. No way, did he want to deal with that. Didn't want her to know he was convinced now that he had made a terrible mistake. Just seeing Mona with his dad had ripped his heart out. He had no one to blame but himself. As he watched Nancy's red lips moving, but he not really hearing, he feigned deep interest in whatever she was jabbering about, nodding here and there and smiling from time to time as though to be listening intently. Had she stopped to ask, he wouldn't have been able to repeat one word of what she had said.

He was grateful, though, when the band began playing one of her favorite Rihanna tunes and he quickly asked her to dance. As he had anticipated, she accepted. He let out a breath of relief. Hopefully, she would shut up for a few minutes while they were on the dance floor. That was something else he had come to realize about her now that they were together, basically, twenty-four-seven – She talked incessantly! It was really beginning to hammer away at his nerves. Sometimes he just wanted to reach out and shut her mouth for her. Anything, to give his ears and nerves some rest. He couldn't do that, though. He just needed to get away from her, but he also needed a little time to work things out for himself. Meanwhile, he had to endure the un-pleasure of Nancy's constant yapping and shallow attitude that he was beginning to see in himself. And he hated it.

On the way home, Michael wanted nothing more than for Mona to invite him inside for a nightcap and perhaps it lead to something more, but as he studied her lovely face, while she talked on with a little more excitement than usual, and what he would have been comfortable with, about her new neighbor, how strange but polite he was and how he had saved her life, Michael couldn't help but notice how she had perked up at the subject of Gavril Canta. He surmised that though she didn't seem to realize it yet, she was interested and probably very attracted to the younger gentleman – though he was older than Darren by about ten years. Michael understood he needed to give her more time.

As much as he wanted her, desired to be with her, she was very young, much younger than he. It would be better for the twenty-two-year-old Mona to be with a man of around thirty-five or so than to be with a man who was quickly approaching fifty-one. That realization kind of stuck with him. He understood at that moment just how much he really cared for her. Though he had never been as shallow or selfish as Darren or Margaret, he had always been somewhat self-centered. He realized the thoughts he was having now were probably the most unselfish he'd ever had in his entire life. The profundity of the realization of how much he actually cared for this young woman almost brought tears to his eyes.

Charlie, his chauffeur, pulled the limousine over to the curb and turned to the couple in the back awaiting instructions.

Surprise was written all over Mona's face when Michael instructed Charlie to wait for him while he escorted Mona to her apartment. It was in stunned silence that she kept looking up at him as he guided her through the store and up the stairs to her apartment. He glanced at the bottom of Gavril's door. The lights were out. The man, very possibly a big rival for Mona's affections, was either out for the evening or in bed asleep. Since it was only five past nine in the evening, Michael assumed the man was out. It was here that he stopped and smiled down at the charmingly perplexed face of Mona. "Yes?"

She flushed slightly; apparently more than a little embarrassed by what she had assumed. "Ah, I just—."

He finished for her. "You expected that I would want to come in."

She nodded yes, still uncomfortable.

He cupped his hand under her chin. "Believe me, Mona. There is nothing I would like better. In fact, I have thought all evening that, if you were willing, I would stay the night. I like you much more than you realize."

"But you've changed your mind?"

"Yes. Yes I have."

"I'm afraid I don't understand. Did I do or say anything to change it?"

"No. You didn't do anything. I simply had time to think about it on the way here. If we get together, I want it to be right. It is too soon since Darren broke up with you. I want to know that our being together is not out of rebound."

"But—."

I want to give you a little more time. Okay?"

"…Okay." Still puzzled, she managed the semblance of a smile.

With a gentle kiss to her forehead, he pulled back. "Now you get a good night's sleep. I'll try to do the same." He smiled, as though laughing at himself. "And I will probably be beating myself up all the way home."

"All right…Although, you don't have to go."

"Yes I do," he stated with resolution. "It's best. You need time, Mona. I think you know it too. Now get some shuteye."

"Yes. I'll do that." She turned to unlock her door.

He stood there until she was inside and the lock clicked. He then adjusted himself inside his trench coat and headed swiftly back down the stairs.

As soon as Michael was gone, Gavril materialized outside Mona's apartment door. He had witnessed everything, heard every word, and taken in every nuance and gesture. Already he had acquired a certain respect for Michael Graves, but at that moment, he had more respect for the gentleman than he'd had for any male human in a very long time. He would definitely think twice before he'd ever harm this man.

Margaret was all decked out in a silvery, sequined evening dress that flattered her five-foot-ten inch, sleek frame that really needed no flattering. Though close to fifty, she was still a vibrantly lovely woman. She was just grabbing her full length, black leather coat out of the closet when Michael arrived. "Going out this late?" he inquired, glancing at his Rolex.

"Come now, Michael…Surely you don't care? And I might ask why you're coming in after nine. But then, I don't really care, either."

He laid his briefcase on the coffee table and slipped out of his jacket. "You're right. I don't. Not as far as you being my wife, that is. You are Darren's mother, though. I'm sure he still loves you. And I still care about the selfish, shallow little twit of a son of ours. So, out of consideration for him, I think we should, at least, know a little about what the other one is doing."

"Okay. Fair enough," She said, pulling her coat together in front and looking him straight in the eyes. "Want to tell me where you were this evening?"

"I took Mona out to dinner. That's all. We had an enjoyable meal and evening. Nothing more and nothing less."

"Mona, really? You mean the young woman Darren was living with?"

"One and the same."

She cocked her head slightly to the side, smugly amused. "You like her! Don't you?"

"Won't lie. Yes I do. However, nothing is going on. I think it's a bit premature to rush into anything, since she and Darren just broke up."

"Not to mention that you're about thirty years her senior."

"More like twenty-nine. However, my birthday is coming up really soon."

"That's right. Do I have to buy you something?" she inquired with a facetious smile.

He rolled his eyes. "No. You don't have to do anything for me. All I ask is that you be there for Darren."

"Not a problem. I love him too." She expelled air. "And, I am going to the Baltic Room with Shane Williams."

Michael couldn't help it. He let out a derisive laugh. "You mean to tell me you're seeing my old enemy Shane with Shane and Richard's?"

"Uh-huh," she replied with a self-satisfied grin, knowing it was a kick in the pants to her husband.

"How long this been going on?"

"Not long…" she replied, grinning mockingly. "In fact, this is our first official date. However, I have met him for lunch a time or two lately."

"All right. Well, you two have fun."

"Don't worry, Michael. I'm sure we will." She moved on to the door and opened it. But before stepping out, she turned and said, "Don't wait up, dear. I might not be home until morning."

With a contemptuous chuckle of resigned acceptance to their relationship, he simply shook his head.

She chortled, slipped out and closed the door. He heard the tumblers fall as she inserted her key and locked the door. It was a habit they all had, locking the door when leaving, even if someone was home. Though theirs was a well-to-do apartment complex, with paid security guards patrolling, there had been some break-ins over the past couple of years. One could not be too careful.

Michael headed straight to the little bar in the corner. A good stiff drink was what he needed right now.

Mona was a little beside herself. Had been all psyched up to have Michael spend the night. Admittedly, at first, she felt a little strange about sleeping with an older man, especially considering the fact that he was the father of her ex-boyfriend. Only, being with him on a more personal level the past few days had made her feel much closer to him. He was physically attractive. She thought the silvery streaks in his dark brown hair very becoming. He had wonderful eyes, shaped just like Darren's. Only Michael's were gray instead of hazel. Although reasoning told her he was doing the right thing, she couldn't help but feel a bit rejected.

Instead of going to bed right away, she poured herself a scotch and soda, turned almost all the lights off, except for the one in the bathroom to give her a little visibility, and dropped into the corner seat of her small sofa, which was more of a loveseat. She sat there sipping on her drink for several minutes, running the evening over and over in her mind. When, suddenly, she had the most vivid vision of Gavril. It was almost as though he were in the room. She immediately sat her glass on the coffee table and leaned forward, eyes scanning the darkened room. In spite of the deep shadows, she could see that she was, indeed, alone. "Crap!" she exclaimed, the vision now gone. "That was so freakin realistic!"

She picked up her drink and scarfed it down. "Think I'll have another." She made her second drink and walked over to the window that looked down at the street and sidewalk below. Headlights shone brightly as the cars moved to and fro. She gasped then, for she had the most powerful feeling. She spun around, half expecting Gavril to be standing there. No one. Just her and the shadows. "Okay. This is getting too weird. Think I've had enough alcohol for one evening. Time for me to get my derriere to bed." She took a quick shower, turned off the bathroom light and slipped in under the bedcovers. The alcohol was working and she fell right to sleep, but the blessed oblivion lasted for only a short time, for she was suddenly standing in a park… No. Not a park, but a cemetery, the same cemetery as before, with that mighty old castle looming in the distance. It was late evening and lightning blazed across the darkening sky. "Dear Lord! Not again!"

Swirling fog caressed her ankles and feet. She was vaguely aware she was dreaming, as the fog rose a little higher, and about a hundred feet away there was a tall shadow, an image, an image of a man – Gavril! His black eyes shone like polished marbles and he wore a black cape that whipped in the wind, not unlike that of Dracula. "What the—?"

In a flash, he stood before her; those black sparkling depths delving down into her very soul. She was completely and utterly mesmerized. She went to speak, but he held a forefinger gently to her lips and shushed her. Then he ever-so-tentatively caressed her cheeks with the tips of his fingers, adoring her. She shivered. He leaned his face in next to hers, their lips all but touching. A transfixing smile came to his face then as he slowly raised his obsidian eyes to hers, piercing her soul once more. "Mona…" he susurrated.

She swallowed hard, unable to speak.

He kissed her forehead and then the tip of her nose and slowly pulled back. "You don't really want to be with Michael, Mona. What you feel for him is more like that of a father. You feel alone and abandoned by Darren, but Michael is not your answer."

She finally found some semblance of voice and asked in a hoarse whisper, "Who are you?"

"You know who I am, Mona. I am Gavril. You may not want to admit it yet, but I have been shadowing your thoughts. Tonight, you were telling Michael about me."

She bobbed her head, agreeing. "Yes. Yes I was talking about you. I've never known anyone quite like you. You're different from anyone I've ever met before."

Pleased by her statement, a satisfied smirk appeared. "Rest assured, I *am* different, Mona. There is no other like me. At least, not around here. I am of a rare kind."

"What do you mean by 'rare kind'?"

For a brief second his eyes turned blood red. She gasped. A deep chuckle welled in his chest. "Do not be afraid of me, Mona. It is not my desire to ever harm you."

Even if she wanted to pull away, she couldn't. She was too captivated by his overpowering presence.

His face grew more serious as he studied her intently. Then totally without warning, he kissed her fully and with unanticipated passion. The profundity of it took a moment to sink into her brain and then she found she could not resist him; and trembling greatly, returned his kiss. In spite of the fiery intensity, there was sweetness in his embrace. The kiss was long and wonderful and she didn't want it to end, but he suddenly ended the kiss just as quickly as it had begun. Speechless now, she gazed upon him in wonderment.

He flashed a secret – bordering on the seductive – smile and disappeared.

Stunned and speechless, she stood there alone in the empty cemetery. "Gavril! Gavril! Where are you, Gavril?"

At once she was awake and sitting up in bed, gasping for air. "God! Oh God! What is happening to me?"

After such an intense dream, Mona had trouble falling back to sleep, but she finally did around four, and even while she slept, visions of Gavril kept wandering in and out of her mind. She was almost glad when the alarm went off at seven. She did her best to push thoughts of her neighbor to the back of her mind and readied for work as quickly as she could, leaving early without taking the time to make coffee. She would grab a Mocha at the Starbucks next to the office building where the law firm was.

Michael was already at the office and on the phone when Mona breezed in, looking well but harried. After he finished his conversation, he took a moment to stick his head in her door. "You okay, Mona?"

Surprised at his question, she shot a look up and replied, "Yes! Why?"

"You just look a little stressed this morning. You sure you're all right?"

"I… I'm good, Michael. Honestly, I had a really weird dream last night. I know it's silly, but it left me a little shook up."

"A nightmare, huh?"

"Ummm…Wouldn't call it a nightmare, exactly. Just strange."

"Want to talk about it?"

Her face relaxed and she let out a little laugh. The dream wasn't exactly one she wanted to share with anyone, especially Michael. "Thank you, Michael. But I'll be okay. Just need to focus on work. I'll be fine."

He smiled approvingly. "That a girl. Because, I need you to know if you can answer some questions for me?"

"Of course. What do you need?"

A strange, unreadable expression crossed his face.

"What?"

"Can you remember back a few weeks ago, right before you and Darren split?"

"Remember what?"

"For instance, August sixteenth. What were you and Darren doing that evening?"

"Huh?" An attractive wrinkle formed on her nose when she spoke with a start. "Why August sixteenth?"

"Just a thought, Mona. Wouldn't even call it a hunch, yet. Still, if you can remember what you and Darren were doing that evening, I'd like to know. Okay?"

"Sure. I'll have to glance at my calendar when I get home. Right now, I couldn't say. I'm afraid I'm not very good with remembering dates."

"No hurry. When you can."

She nodded, indicating that she would do it, and he went on.

Briefly, Michael considered asking Mona out to dinner again, and then rethought it. Though every part of him wanted to be with her, the fact that he could see she was attracted to someone else, whether she realized it or not, was a great deterrent in his desires to be with her. It was only a matter of time before she would come to realize it herself.

Then there was the other problem – namely his son. It wasn't the slight signs of jealousy he was seeing from his offspring that was troubling Michael. He figured Darren deserved losing Mona's affections now. No. It was something else, something more troubling. He had known for some time that Darren was spoiled. Only he hadn't realized just how rotten his son was until recently. Now he had a nagging feeling that just would not go away.

He kept telling himself he was wrong. Still, it was troubling him more and more daily. Part of him didn't want to know, but the other part, the lawyer in him, had to know. Was his son guilty of something more sinister than being a womanizer and irresponsible jerk? He hoped not. Still, he had to find out. That was why he had asked Mona what she and Darren had been doing the evening of August sixteenth. If she could come back with a definite answer, that they were together that evening, then it would set his mind at ease. He hoped, oh how he hoped, that she could.

Darren was glad Nancy wanted to go tanning after work. He hoped it would give him the opportunity to speak to Mona. He couldn't help but notice that his dad and Mona had appeared to be all business through the day. Had they had a disagreement? A fight, perhaps? He couldn't help it. He hoped so. It was getting to the point that he didn't even want to be around Nancy's smugness and incessant chattering anymore. What he had once perceived as somewhat attractive self-assuredness, he now looked upon as just plain cold-hearted, self-centeredness. He had no doubts whatsoever that she was convinced that she had him hook, line and sinker. Sure, she had displayed some signs of jealousy, but he felt it was more in wanting to be the center of attention than real jealousy. She didn't love him, nor did he love her, at least, not anymore.

He realized that he really might not be any better than Nancy, but seeing the ugliness in her, kind of mirrored his own faults back. That, he did not like. Made him uncomfortable and he hated it. Soon as she was gone, he was out the door. He hoped that Mona's neighbor wasn't around. There was a creepiness about that guy that gave him the willies.

Darren glanced at the bottom of Mona's neighbor's door. The lights were on. *Shit!* He hesitated briefly, but he could hear Mona moving around in her apartment, probably getting herself something to eat. Finally gathering up the courage, he knocked lightly on her door, hoping not to catch unwanted attention from across the hall.

All got silent for a moment, and then the door swung open. Mona stood there, already dressed in her casual wear, black sweatshirt and jeans. "I'm just about to eat my dinner, Darren."

Anxiously, he glanced at the door across the way and then turned back to Mona. "Can I come in for a minute?"

"Seriously?" she sniggered cynically.

"Please!"

She exhaled loudly. "Oh… All right." She stepped aside for him to enter.

He let out a sigh of relief, for he had the weirdest feeling he was being watched out in the hall. "Thanks, Mona."

She headed towards her small kitchen. "I'd offer you something, but then I really don't want you to stay."

"It's okay, Mona. I don't blame you for feeling the way you do. I just came here to tell you how terribly sorry I am."

Unmoved, she replied, "You know that I don't believe a damn word that comes out of your mouth anymore?"

He shut his eyes momentarily, desperately trying to hold back any anger. This was what he deserved. Opening his eyes again, he said. "I got it, Mona. What I did to you was unforgivable. I feel like the low, sorry sonovabitch that I was to you. But please believe me when I tell you that I really am sorry."

Just then, they heard the door across the hall open.

Darren gulped. "Does that guy have radar or something?" he asked, with a back tilt of his head.

"He's a gentleman, Darren. He's just making sure you don't get out of line."

"But you're not his business, Mona," Darren sharply replied.

She screwed up her mouth and shook her head slowly from side to side. "You would see it that way. Like I said, *he's* a gentleman. Something I am sure you haven't a clue how to be."

Holding palms up in front of himself, Darren did his best to stifle his rising anger. "Okay… I came here to apologize, Mona. I don't want to fight."

"All right. Apology accepted. Now please go."

"I will. Only, I want to add that I know now that leaving you for Nancy was the biggest mistake I ever made in my entire life."

Her face softened marginally, as she believed he was actually being truthful. "Okay, Darren. Like I said, I accept your apology, but it's over. It hurt like hell, but I'm moving on."

"With my father?"

"I don't know." She gesticulated with a shrug. "Maybe. Maybe not. That remains to be seen."

"Okay." With a reluctant but agreeable nod, he turned and went to the door, only to briefly face Mona again. "Thanks for letting me come in."

"Not a problem."

Sure enough, when Darren opened the door, Gavril was in the hall peering out the window that viewed out over the front of the building. He turned towards Darren, but his face was stoic and eyes unreadable.

Darren muttered, "Evening."

"Evening," Gavril icily replied.

Darren literally ran down the hall and to the stairwell where he could be heard stumbling his way down the stairs, wasting not a second in exiting the building.

When Mona went to the door to close it, as Darren had left it ajar, her eyes met Gavril's midnight depths. Recollections of the dream she'd had the previous night flooded back to her in a torrent. For some crazy, inexplicable reason, she sensed he knew about the dream. His face was no longer stoic, and his eyes danced with fascinating little lights. She flushed, remembering the passionate kiss in her dream. Not sure how to handle what was transpiring, she uttered, "Good evening."

"Evening, Mona… Pleasant dreams."

Her jaw dropped. His barely detectable, self-assured smile said it all. He knew! She rushed in and swiftly closed her door, leaning her back up against it. "Oh my God! Oh my God! Who and what is he?"

Harry was handing over a bagged prescription to an elderly gentleman when Darren dashed through the store and out the door as though the building were on fire. Harry glanced questioningly to his wife who was decorating the display window. Both shared a puzzled look. Even the customer remarked, "Guess the young man is in a hurry."

"Must be," Harry responded.

When the customer was gone, Harry suggested to Matilda that maybe she should check on Mona.

"Just what I was thinking," she replied and headed up the stairs to Mona's apartment.

Though back inside his own apartment, Gavril heard Matilda trudging up the stairs. The older woman was concerned about Mona. That was good. He was glad their landlords cared about their tenants. He poured himself a drink and eased down in the recliner. He would hear every word, even though both apartment doors were closed.

Mona all but jumped out of her skin when Matilda suddenly rapped on her door. "Mona? You okay, hon?"

"Oh shit!" she replied, touching a hand to her chest with a gasp. "Yes! Yes. I'm okay." She flung the door open.

Matilda frowned slightly. "You don't look okay. You can tell me, you know."

There was no way she could explain what was going on between her and the mysterious man across the hall. She didn't understand it herself. She had to think of something, though. "Darren…" she managed. "Darren came up to apologize for the awful way he did me. Still, I really didn't want to talk to him. Kind of shook me up."

"Ha!" the older woman sniggered sardonically. "You mean he actually apologized?" she asked, stepping in as Mona made way for her to enter.

"Believe it or not, he did."

"You think he really is sorry?"

Mona sat down to her little kitchen table that rested up against the left side of the refrigerator and had two chairs. "Truthfully, I do."

Matilda took the other seat, scrutinizing Mona's face. "I'm sorry that little jerk has you so upset. If you want, I can call the police the next time he shows up here?"

"It's okay. I'm not so sure he'll be back."

"Yeah…" she grinned as though something funny suddenly came to mind. "He was in a mighty hurry when he left, now that I think about it." She turned to face Mona straight on. "Something happen?"

Mona reflected her grin. "Kind of."

Matilda reached over a hand and patted Mona's. "What?"

"He's afraid of Gavril."

"Oh! Really?" she grinned hugely. "What happened?"

"We heard Gavril's door open. It made Darren nervous. Anyway, when Darren went to leave, Gavril was there in the hall. I… I think he was listening to our conversation. All it took was one look from Gavril and Darren ran out of here like a pack of wolves was on his tail."

Chuckling now, Matilda said, "Yes. We definitely noticed that. The running out of here, that is. Did Gavril say anything to him?"

"Just good evening. I think it was more Gavril's visage than the conversation that got to Darren. I think Darren is intimidated by the man. Clearly, Gavril doesn't like him."

"Good for Gavril! Honestly, I never said anything when you were with Darren, but I never really liked the little jerk much. But you loved him, so I kept my mouth shut."

"I kind of picked up on that. Honestly, part of me knew the truth. I just didn't want to believe it."

"Yes. It's human nature to want to believe in the people we care about." Her expression changed as though an idea just occurred to her. "Gavril… Do you like him?"

Mona was a little surprised by the question. She'd been trying so hard not to think about the dream she'd had the night before. "…He saved my life."

Matilda gave her another pat on the hand. "And he's *really* good-looking, isn't he?" She smiled naughtily.

Mona glanced around, embarrassed. She cleared her throat. "Now that you mention it…" she admitted with a grin.

Laughing harder. "I thought so. You do find him attractive. What woman in her right mind wouldn't? He is – as you young folks say these days – hot!" She fanned her face, chuckling. "Whew! Don't ever tell Harry I said that."

"Don't worry. I won't tell. Promise."

"I didn't think you would. You know I love my man. That doesn't mean I can't appreciate a fine looking gentleman when I see one. He's like a magnificent work of art." She blew out air. "And one would have to be freakin' dead not to appreciate that one."

Both cackled.

"Well," she said, standing from the table. "I'd best get down there or Harry will think something *is* wrong."

"Okay. Thanks for coming up to see about me."

"Not a problem, sweetie. You just let me know if you need anything."

"Thank you, Matilda."

"I'll let myself out. Have a good evening."

"You too."

It was ten p.m. when Michael took his shower and donned his maroon, silk bathrobe that Margaret had given him for last Christmas. He sniggered to himself. Funny, though they had been married in name only for the past ten years or so, she always bought him nice gifts at Christmas and for his birthday, as though she cared.

It was the front she felt necessary to present. Had to let her friends know what a wonderful wife she was to her hardworking lawyer of a husband. Little did they know what a true bitch she actually was. Still, to her social circle and Facebook friends, she was the epitome of what a good wife should be. He let his wife have her little charade. She was content with it, as long as she could spend his money and keep up her social appearances. It wasn't for her sake that he let her little pretense continue; it was and had been mainly for Darren and Richard. Only both were grown men now: Richard, their eldest, on the other side of the states with his wife and son, and Darren here, practicing with the firm. Had been for some time now, and Michael was tired of the false front everyone displayed. It was downright ridiculous.

Little did Margaret know just how close she could be to losing it all. He knew all to well how the social circles functioned. Right now she was the center of attention of many of her friends, but the moment he filed for divorce and they separated, she would no longer be in much demand. She'd be a loner at social gatherings, more of a has-been. Her fair-weather friends would stop inviting her to all their gatherings and her social life would quickly fade away into oblivion. That is unless she found a way to make it into the upper classes on her own and not by marriage. If she became a best-selling author or something along that line, then she would be able to maintain her social status, but he knew Margaret. She didn't aspire to working for anything other than winning a game of Bridge.

For Michael, it would only take Mona displaying what he knew to be genuine affections towards him to make it all happen; affections that he knew were sincere and not fabricated. Unlike Margaret, Mona actually had the ability to care about people besides herself and her offspring.

Michael's thoughts were interrupted by a sudden chill; felt like someone opened a window. He sat forward on the sofa, placed his half-empty nightcap on the coffee table and stood. He tightened the belt on his robe and walked over to the big windows that looked out over the city. Closed. "Weird." He walked back through the living room and into the kitchen. All the windows there were shut. Again, a definite draft. "What the hell—?" Maybe he was coming down with a cold. "Gads. Last thing I need. Can't afford to take time off right now."

The lights suddenly flickered. He decided that maybe a storm was coming. He peered out the big windows again. "Nope. Just a few clouds. Can actually see some stars. Unless it's coming from the south." With that thought, he hurried off to his and Margaret's bedroom and looked out the window there. No storm clouds. "Huh! Strange indeed."

Sudden darkness. It took a second to register in his brain. "Okay…" There was a flashlight in a bottom drawer in the kitchen. Visibility was just enough from the glow of city lights – *lights* – outside the building to make his way to the kitchen and get the flashlight. Once he had it and switched it on, he went to the door and opened it. The hall was dark. He could hear people in the elevator and at first thought that they were stuck, but the door slid open and a shaft of light shown out of the elevator into the dark hall. The surprised tenants couldn't believe it when they stepped out.

"What's going on?" Rex Taylor, the young African American man that lived down the hall, asked, as the two lovely black girls with him stepped up by his side.

"Hell if I know," Michael replied. "My lights just went out… Not five minutes ago. Are they on in the rest of the building?"

"Hell yeah!"

"Is it windy out?"

"Not at all. We just came up."

"I'll call maintenance. Surely they can tell us what's going on."

"We'll wait," the young man replied.

He pulled his cell phone out of his robe pocket and selected building maintenance. George Holtz, the janitor, was completely surprised when he heard about the power outage. Said he'd get right on it. Sure enough, the lights were back on almost instantly. Somehow a switch had been thrown. He seemed aghast as to how it had happened and apologized for the inconvenience. Michael told him not to worry about it. The power was back on. Sometimes things just happen. After thanking the janitor, he dropped his phone back in his pocket and switched his flashlight off.

With a thumbs-up from Rex, he and his lady friends disappeared into his apartment.

No one noticed the tall shadow in the shape of a man evaporate at the end of the hall.

Nancy sat at the little bar that joined the kitchen and living room. She'd been quietly observing Darren for the past half hour. He was on the sofa in front of their sixty-five inch plasma television, feet propped up on the coffee table, but he wasn't really watching television. He wasn't himself, definitely agitated about something, but she couldn't put a finger on it. Was he lying? Could it be he was actually having real regrets for having dumped Mona for her? She couldn't see how that was possible, when she compared herself with Mona.

Mona was pretty and nice, the girl next door type, too nice at times, sometimes sweet to the point of being downright sickening, but she didn't have the drive, the ambition, the knowhow that it took to be the wife of a successful lawyer such as Darren or his father, or any other lawyer that Nancy knew personally. No. Mona struck her as more the docile little female who was more than anxious to please with no true dreams or aspirations of her own. Or, if she did have any, Nancy had seen no clues of it.

Mona was the kind of female that Nancy had no respect for. Though somewhat rare these days, she came off as being an old-fashioned girl, just working to support herself until she could land herself a husband to take care of her and any future offspring they might have, the very kind of woman Nancy simply could not stomach.

Darren finished off the beer he'd been nursing and rose from the sofa, the back of which faced Nancy at the bar. He turned his head and flashed an unimpressive smile. Her eyes did not leave him while he slowly made his way to the refrigerator and took out another beer.

"What's wrong with you?" she suddenly blurted, unable to stand the oh-so-boring silence any longer.

He jerked his head around, surprised by her outburst. "Say what?'

"Darren! You're not yourself! There's something going on with you that you are not owning up to. What the hell is it?"

He thought about it for a moment while he uncapped his beer and tossed the cap in the garbage under the sink and then turned and took a long drink of his beer, killing almost half of it before taking it from his lips. "A number of things, Nancy."

"Care to share? That's what I'm here for."

He snickered at that.

"What's so funny?"

"Sorry. That was rude."

"Yes it was...What gives, Darren?"

"I'm sorry, Nancy. It's just hard for me to perceive you as the type that really cares about my feelings."

"Darren! That hurts!"

"You're got to admit, Nancy, that you're not exactly the sensitive type."

"I'll grant that. But I am your girlfriend. And as hard as it may be for you to believe, I do want to be here for you. So tell me what's wrong. Please!"

He went over and sat down on the stool next to her. "For one, the Harrison case."

"Yes. You told me about that. What else?"

He took another long sip of his beer, eyes fixed on hers until he sat his bottle down on the bar. "You're an outstanding woman, Nancy. You're a go-getter. And, you're beautiful."

"But—?" She said with emphasis.

"I just think that we jumped into moving in together a little too soon."

"You sonovabitch!" she stood, nostrils flaring angrily. "You do want Mona back, don't you?"

He held up a hand. "No! No...No...No...You misunderstand. Mona doesn't want me back, Nancy."

"Humph! But you want her. Right?"

"No," he lied. She would make life hell for him if she thought she was being dumped. And, it was true, Mona didn't want him back. Nancy was no more to blame for that than he. "Sit down. Please?" he said, looking up at her in as pleasant and pleading a face he could muster.

"All right." She blew out air and sat back down.

"I am still worried about the Harrison case. Afraid my dad will find out I kept things from him."

"Uh-huh. Why do I get the feeling there is something else too?"

"Even though I am with you now…" He put out a hand and laid it over hers, "and I *am* with you now, Nancy, I feel badly about the way I did Mona. Even I have to admit it was sudden. It does look a little weird that I moved out of her apartment and right in with you. I've gotten a snide comment or two from Bill Grayson about it. Also, I have to confess that I am a little concerned about a new neighbor she has."

Nancy's brow furrowed. "Who cares about Bill Grayson? And what about Mona's new neighbor?"

"I think I mentioned him to you before."

"You said something to the effect that you thought he was a little weird."

"Let me correct myself. He's more than a little weird. Make that a lot. Frankly, he scares me a little."

"Wait a minute! You've been going over there!" Her eyes flashed angrily again and she stood.

"Jeeze! I wish you wouldn't fly off the handle like that without letting me finish."

She huffed but sat back down. "Okay… Finish."

"I did. But it wasn't to try and get her back. Nothing like that. Like I said, I just feel kind of like a jerk for dumping her so suddenly the way I did. I just wanted to tell her. So, I did."

Nancy was listening, but she wasn't happy. "So? Anything else?" she snapped.

"I'm done with her. Promise."

Nancy was dubious. It was ingrained in her cold stare.

"But that neighbor must be watching her like a hawk. He was in the hall when I left, Nancy. And the looks that man gave me –!" He began to shake just recalling the incident."

It was so obvious that Nancy couldn't help but notice. "My God! You're trembling, Darren!"

"Believe me, Nancy. I have no intentions of ever going by there again. Still, I can't help but wonder if Mona is safe there."

She thought about it for a minute. "Okay. It would be really cold of me not to consider the safety of another human being. I hope she's not in any danger from this man. Also, I am sure many would find it commendable that you are concerned for her welfare. However, you broke up with her. She is not your concern anymore."

"Of course, you're right." He wasn't about to argue the issue with her any further. Still, he couldn't help but wonder. He did care about Mona's welfare. But he cared for his own, too.

"Here's a thought."

"What?"

"Tell you what. Your dad has shown a definite interest in Mona. You tell him about your concerns with her new neighbor." She raised an eyebrow. "Okay? Get my drift?"

"Okay. You're right. My dad can check on her."

"Good. Now, why don't you take me to Outback for a steak? It's a little late for preparing anything ourselves. And, hopefully, there won't be a crowd at dinner… now that it's bedtime!"

He glanced at his watch. It was after ten. "Damn! I had no idea it was that late. Steak sounds good. Just let me slip into jeans."

"Thank you, Darren," she said as he rose from his stool.

"For what?" He'd never known her to thank anyone in any truly meaningful way before.

"For telling me what has been troubling you. I was afraid you wanted to leave me."

He snorted a laugh. "No! Of course not!" he lied. "We're good." He smiled as sincerely as he could feign and went off to change.

Chapter Five:

Harry had made a run to the bank to make a night deposit and Matilda was just closing down the drugstore; white shade already drawn over the front glass door, when a couple of young men with black stockings over their heads slipped in unnoticed, surprising her just as she was locking up the register. They were on her so fast she didn't have time to try and get away. The taller one poked a gun into her ribs and ordered her to open the register back up, while the other went to raking as many bottles of various drugs as he could find into a black cloth bag.

"I... I can't!" she replied, telling the truth. Harry had the master key, and once the register was locked up, it couldn't be opened up again without it.

"I said open the register!" the man ordered, shoving the end of the gun barrel even harder into her ribs, causing her to cry out.

The shorter man had his bag filled and came around to Matilda's other side. "Better do as he says, ma'am. He's not a man of patience."

"I'm telling you that I can't," she insisted, tears of fear now webbing down her face. "My husband has the key."

"Where's your husband?"

"He's not here."

"We don't have time for this," the taller one said. "Find something to pry the register open."

The shorter man sat the bag aside and began searching down the aisles for something that they could use.

Matilda stood there, terrified, staring into the unmoving green eyes that stared back at her through two holes. Then her eyes shifted slightly as another man suddenly appeared, as though out of thin air, right behind him – Mr. Conta.

Noticing the expression on Matilda's face, the would-be robber turned to see what Matilda was staring at. A man with the coldest black eyes he'd ever seen. Something innate told him he was in trouble. He let out a little yelp as he went sailing across the store, meeting the far wall with a hard thump and dropping to the floor with a clunk.

Seeing what had happened to his partner, the shorter man yelled, "Jesus!" And didn't hesitate, ran out the front door, only to find himself face to face with Gavril around the corner. "How in hell—?"

It took Matilda a minute to realize what had taken place. All had transpired so quickly. The taller man was lying crumpled in the floor moaning. Just then, Harry came in, immediately seeing something was wrong. It took him only a second to realize there had been an attempted robbery, but his first concern was for his wife, who was obviously very glad to see him, judging by her bright, relieved smile.

"Mr. Conta stopped them, Harry," she said, eyes big as saucers. "I've never seen anything like it in my entire life."

He took his wife in his arms and held her shaking body. Just then, Gavril walked in the store with the second robber, who was white as a sheet, having had the stocking removed, but being more than cooperative. Gavril ordered him to stay with Harry, who was now on his cell phone calling the police. The man on the floor was slowly coming around. When he saw Gavril, he screamed and scrambled to his knees in a feeble attempt to flee, but Gavril was much too quick and was at once before him.

"Going someplace?"

The man shook his head and sputtered, "No! No! Not going anywhere."

"Good."

Having heard some of the commotion, Mona slipped into her jeans and a sweatshirt and went down to see what was going on. "Oh my God!" Her focus went to Matilda who still clung to her husband. "What happened?"

In his calm but distinct voice, Gavril answered, "These two gentlemen thought they were going to rob Harry and Matilda here. However, I believe I've convinced them that stealing is not a safe profession to take on."

The taller man's head vibrated up and down, agreeing with Gavril. The shorter man was apparently speechless. Just then, two police cars pulled up in front, red and blue lights flashing. Four officers rushed inside with guns drawn, but when they saw that all was under control, they holstered them.

Captain Phillips, a big burly man, had the black female cop with him handcuff the taller man, and a young male rookie with blond hair handcuffed the shorter one. Phillip's asked Gavril what had happened, but Gavril indicated with a nod to Matilda. "I believe you should talk to the young lady there, Officer Phillips. She's the one they attempted to rob."

"Yeah… But you're the one who stopped them!" Matilda said, admiring her hero.

"In that case," Phillips said, "Please stick around. I may have some questions for you."

Gavril replied, "Certainly." His eyes went to Mona then, as she was staring at him in wonder now. He went up to her. "Sorry if we woke you. Did we?"

"Why are you apologizing? You obviously did a wonderful thing here."

"Perhaps," he replied, eyes fixed on hers. "Still, I would hate to think I was responsible for disturbing your rest."

"Not at all."

Harry came over and laid a hand on Gavril's shoulder. "Mr. Conta, I owe you big time. You saved my wife. You saved our money – everything. We owe you!"

Gavril took it all in as though he'd done nothing out of the ordinary. "Just doing what any decent gentleman would do, Harry. I can call you Harry, right?"

"Of course!" Harry gave him a buddy slap. "Damn right! You can call me Harry. In fact," he said, screwing his mouth around as though an idea came to him, "I don't want you paying any rent while you're here."

"That's really nice of you to offer," Gavril replied, "but I can't let you do that."

"Yes you can! I insist. I don't want a dime from you as long as you are here."

"Well… Since you insist, how can I say no?"

Phillip's made his way over. The other officers were escorting the two hoodlums out the door. "Can I have that word with you now, Mr. Canta?"

"Certainly," Gavril replied and excused himself from Harry, Mona and Matilda who had just walked up to join them.

Matilda said she was exhausted and just wanted to go upstairs. Harry told her to go on up, he'd be there as soon as he could close the store.

"You coming?" Matilda asked Mona.

"In a little," Mona replied. "I'd like to speak with Mr. Conta first."

"Ok, hon. Night."

"Night."

Gavril heard and smiled secretively to Mona over Officer Phillip's shoulder. Mona couldn't contain her grin. She turned, a little embarrassed, and pretended to be looking at the cosmetic display.

"Well," Harry said, "I'm going to finish up here and lock up soon as Officer Phillips leaves."

"Yes. Go ahead." Mona leaned back against the counter then to wait for Gavril. She let herself take a good look at him, something she'd intentionally tried to avoid up until now, because of the way he made her feel, which was kind of wild and kind of crazy and kind of wonderful, and yet, a little scary. There was something very deep and mysterious about him. She sensed something dark, something very dark. It terrified and thrilled her at the same time.

At last, Phillips wrapped up and left out the door. Gavril turned and reached for Mona's hand. "Shall we?" he asked, with a nod towards the back stairs.

"Yes." She accepted his hand and instantly realized it was cold.

He seemed to know what she was thinking. "Sorry. I suffer from a slight condition. Hope you don't mind? My hands are always cold. But, to risk boring you with an old cliché, you know what they say – 'Cold hands, warm heart'." His eyes sparkled.

She grinned, but found it hard to find a comment that wouldn't make her sound like a complete idiot. His mere presence tended to unravel her through and through. When they reached the top of the stairs, he said, "You mentioned that you wanted to talk to me."

"Yes."

"Would you like to come in to my apartment? Or would you prefer I come in to yours? Or do you just want to speak with me here in the hall?"

Something told her that if she were smart, she would insist on staying in the hall, but she didn't want to be smart. She tingled all over simply by being near him. And that scent, that awesome scent – pine, sage, herbs of the forest. She spoke before thinking it through, "That scent. What is it? You smell absolutely awesome."

The little lights in his eyes danced with amusement. "Nothing in particular. It's just who I am." A light chuckle. "Glad you like the way I… smell."

Now she was really embarrassed. Her face flushed hot. "I'm sorry! Oh my God! I must seem like a silly schoolgirl."

On the contrary, he replied, still holding her hand. He gently squeezed her fingers and then released her hand.

She couldn't help but gaze into those black, resplendent depths. Someone sighed, and she realized that it was she. His eyes fell to her lips and then he suddenly kissed her, sweetly, tenderly, passionately. It took her only a brief second to respond, returning his kiss more than willingly. His lips found her neck and he gently kissed her warm flesh there. Then she felt something besides his lips, felt like teeth, but it was only for a fleeting second. He pulled away from her then, eyes beholding hers. "I'm sorry. You did say you wanted to talk to me. It is just that I find you very attractive," he let his eyes play over her body, "and I kind of let my reserve down. My sincere apologies." His smile was ambiguous as he let his eyes come to rest on her face.

Breathless, she wasn't certain how to respond. "Oh… It's okay," she replied, following his every move with her own eyes.

"Shall we?" He held out a hand, indicating to his apartment.

Everything in her common sense screamed no, but she nodded yes, knowing full well that there was something very different about him. Still, she could not help herself. Her desire to know him far outweighed her instinct telling her to beware of this man. Eagerly, she stepped inside – An innocent school girl accepting a stranger's offer of candy.

He was right behind her and ever so quietly closed the door. Once it was shut, he held out a hand, encouraging her to go on into his living room. He offered her a drink, but she declined. He offered her a seat on the sofa, which she took. He joined her, turning and cupping her chin in his hand, all the while studying her face like a fine work of art. "You may speak, Mona."

Though she could not pull away from his mesmerizing stare, she finally managed to speak, "I just wanted to thank you. You not only saved my life, you have now saved Matilda from what would probably have been an awful fate, and you saved the both of them financially. I just wanted to tell you, I think you are absolutely wonderful."

"And you like the way I smell," he added, grinning enticingly.

She couldn't help it. She blurted, "What is it about you? You're not like anyone else I've ever known. You don't seem to be afraid of anything or anyone. What's more, you have this mind-blowing composure. Is there anything that scares you? Is there anything that ever gets to you?"

"Ah… sweet Mona." He gently placed his palms to her cheeks, holding his face close to hers. "I have been around a very long time. Very settled in my ways. Old-fashioned, one might say." He kissed the tip of her nose, pulled back and continued, "As you say, I am not like anyone else you know. Therefore, I must warn you, I can be… I am… very dangerous to anyone who happens to cross my path at the wrong time."

Her brow furrowed. "Are you telling me… you've killed people?"

He almost seemed amused by her question, stifling a smug grin. "Yes. Yes, Mona. I've killed a number of people in my long life."

Less sure of him now, she pulled back slightly.

Responding to her reaction, he said, "I would never hurt you. You are beautiful... considerate of others… sweet. Not selfish and self-centered like so many. I hope the fact that I have killed a time or two won't stop you from liking me. Does it?"

Half apologetic, bewildered, she replied, "I don't know the facts, Gavril. Were you in a war? A police officer, perhaps? Did you have reason and justification in killing them?"

"I had my reasons. And I had my justifications. However, my justifications might not be the same as yours in a given situation."

She stuttered, confused. He seemed to talk in riddles. "I… I fail to understand, Gavril. You have been nothing but awesome, from what I've witnessed. I get the feeling you are trying to tell me something here. Can't you just come out and say it?"

"I could." He stood and moved to his little make-shift bar on the kitchen table. He held up a glass. "Would you care for a drink?"

"Do you have a beer?"

"Sure." He grabbed one out of the small refrigerator that was to the left of the table (one he'd just purchased for his alcoholic beverages) and pulled the cap off with his fingers.

Amazed, she stared at the bottle and then him, as he walked over and handed it to her. "How did you do that?"

"You should know by now, Mona. I'm very strong."

"I know what you did downstairs. But you just pulled a bottle cap off with your bare fingers! Didn't it hurt?"

Grinning that mysterious grin of his, he answered, "Not a bit." He sat back down by her.

Both sipped on their drinks for a few minutes, exchanging glances, considering one another.

After a bit, Mona sat her half drank beer down on his coffee table, turned and looked at him questioningly. "Did you want to… bite me earlier?"

"You picked up on that." He grinned as though he were proud of himself.

Somewhat bewildered, she asked, "Why in hell would you want to bite me?"

His response was not what she expected. "I would like to make love to you."

Her jaw gaped as she sat there silently letting his words sink in. She didn't know what to say. She desired him, desired him something fierce, and the longer she sat there with him beholding her in his inviting stare, the more she wanted him. *"Oh God!"* she gasped.

Instantly, he was upon her, kissing her, caressing her, fondling her. She had no strength to resist. "My sweet Mona," he whispered, now kissing her neck again, "I am a vampire." Then he held a hand over her mouth while he bit into her soft flesh. She struggled, but only briefly, at last surrendering her will to his. He drank and fondled her as he drank, and then, just on the verge of her passing out, he ripped open his wrist and placed it over her mouth. She tried to refuse, but was too weak and he insisted. "I don't want you to die, young lady. My blood will strengthen you. If you don't drink, you *will* die." That did sink in. Immediately, she complied, sucking at his wrist with surprising thirst. "There... You see. It's really quite easy." He let her drink for a few more moments, and then pulled his wrist away. He sucked the remaining blood off his wrist.

To her amazement, his wound healed in front of her eyes. She sat there staring at him, blood dripping down her chin, confused and dazed, not knowing what to do or think.

"Stay there. I'll get something to tidy you up." He vanished into thin air.

Stunned again, she remained seated.

He was back in a few seconds with a clean, wet washcloth. He washed off her mouth and chin and then his own and sat the cloth aside. "Now, feel all better?"

Eyes glued to his, her head vibrated yes.

He gently gathered her in his arms as though she were his long lost child that he'd finally found, and held her lovingly. "It is not my desire to harm you. Unfortunately, the vampire's bite stings a little. For that, I apologize." He kissed the top of her head.

She finally found her voice to speak. "You really are a vampire." Her eyes went up to his questioningly. "I always thought vampires were fictional… But you really *are* a vampire!" She was trying very hard to fathom what was happening.

"Yes I am, my sweet. However, it must remain our little secret. Tell no one."

"I won't. After all you've done for me… for my friends. I'll never tell anyone."

"That's my girl." He skewed his head back slightly. Although he knew, he asked anyway, "You *are* my girl now, aren't you?"

"I am?"

He chuckled. "Are you?"

"Are you saying you want me to be your girlfriend?"

"Not my girlfriend, Mona. I want you for my mate."

She coughed and cleared her throat before speaking, "Your mate?"

"I know this is a lot for you to assimilate so fast. For that, I apologize too."

"I sense it implies something other than being a girlfriend?"

"Yes. It does. A mate is a permanent status. Girlfriends can come and go."

"Ok. I understand… I think."

"There is nothing more I want than to make love to you, Mona. However, I will give you a little more time. I want to allow my blood time to work in your veins. You will notice some changes. They won't be major, but they *will* be noticeable. This will give you time to think about things."

"I don't fully understand. But… okay. I guess."

He stood and offered her a hand and assisted her in rising. "Now, I suggest you return to your apartment and get a good night's sleep. And," he grinned smugly, "you might have some really bizarre dreams. In fact, you most likely will."

"Oh!" It hit her. "You! You sent me those dreams, didn't you?"

"Guilty," he replied with a self-satisfied smirk.

"I thought I was losing my freakin' mind."

"Now you know you're not."

He escorted her to her apartment door and kissed her quickly and returned to his own, closing his door before she was fully inside. That was when she heard his voice, clearly and distinctly, in her head say, "Lock your door." She did. Then she smiled to herself. "That was cool." Confused but happy, she went to bed.

She lay in the dark for some time, going over and over everything in her mind: how she felt about Michael, how she felt about Darren, and most of all how she felt about Gavril, whom she had just learned was a vampire. She understood that he had some kind of hold over her, some kind of power, but she didn't care. She tingled from head to foot, and her breasts swelled with warmth. The more she thought about him, the more she wanted him to make love to her; wanted – craved – for him to come take her in his arms. She shivered and thrilled at the thought. Finally, she rolled over, tired, and managed to fall asleep.

Michael was on his way out the door when he stopped in the living room. Margaret had the early morning news on. "You might want to see this, Michael," she said. "Isn't that the drugstore where Mona's Sims apartment is? I was there once, when Mona and Darren were together."

Michael recognized Harry Butler right away. He was talking to the newswoman, holding up a microphone to his face. Michael sat his briefcase back down. "What's going on?"

"Looks like there was an attempted holdup late yesterday evening, but one of their tenants stopped it in progress."

Mona was seen trying to make her way through the reporters to get out the door. "I didn't really see anything," she quickly responded to the reporter, now trying to get a statement out of her. "I just know what Mrs. Butler said. That Mr. Conta intervened and stopped the two men."

"Would you know where Mr. Conta is now? He didn't answer when we knocked on his door."

"I have no idea," Mona said. "I have to get to work. I'm sorry." She ran on out the door.

Michael retrieved his briefcase. "And I need to get to work. Let me know if they come up with anything more."

"Sure," Margaret replied.

Brow slightly furrowed, as though something suddenly came to mind, he stopped at the door. "I thought you were going to spend the night with Shane?"

"I was. But I changed my mind. Decided I'd be more comfortable here."

"Okay… Well, have a good day."

"You too, dear," she said with a slightly mocking tone.

Michael figured his wife must have had a falling out with her new lover, or she wouldn't be home this early. "Oh well…" he breathed and headed on out to his car. It didn't really matter to him anymore. Mona was the only woman he desired now, but he had the distinct feeling it wasn't going to happen.

Mona couldn't wait to get to work. She'd had one of the strangest nights in her entire life. As Gavril had promised, she had dreams all right, many dreams; one would finish and go right into another, but they all, basically, had the same theme. She dreamed of that old but beautiful castle. It seemed to be right out the stories of Dracula. There were bats flying in and out of her visions and wolves howling balefully at the moon. There were cemeteries, ancient crypts and tombstones and heavy fog drifting here and there. Then, in the midst of it all, she would see a tall dark shadow standing with a dark cape whipping in the wind, but it wasn't Dracula, it was Gavril, and he held out a hand to her and bid her to come, come and fly away with him. "Come be with me and ride the back of forever."

"I don't know," she would say, but knew deep down that she wanted to be with him more than anything. Still, he frightened her. He frightened her beyond measure. The dreams were equally beautiful and nightmarish, lingering in her thoughts. "God!" she gasped, as she stepped out of the elevator alone. It had been empty, of which she was glad. "Just help me get through today," she whispered. "Just get me through today. Then, maybe tonight, I'll be able to think more clearly."

She was so far off in thought when she rushed past Michael's desk on the way to her little side office that she failed to even notice that he was already there. He noticed her, though. Stood immediately and followed her inside.

"Hey… You okay?" he asked, as she realized he was right behind her and turned around.

"Honestly, Michael, I don't know." She stood there for a moment not knowing what to say or do. She was so confused, so confounded. But here was this handsome older man, one she looked up to and admired greatly, one who cared deeply for her, and she just let loose. The tears gushed forth, and she just could not contain herself.

Immediately, he enfolded her in his arms, gently stroking her shoulder-length hair down the back. He had no clue as to the true nature of her plight. He could only assume that it had to do with the attempted burglary of the evening before. With his free arm, he reached back and closed the door behind them, so no one could hear. "I'm here, Mona. I'm here." He held her for several minutes, letting her cry it all out.

She finally managed to quit sobbing and sniffled, pulling back, all apologetic. "I'm sorry. I've gotten the lapel of your suit all wet."

"I don't give a damn about this suit, Mona. It will dry. You are the only thing I truly care about."

Sniffling again, "Still… This is your office. I… I shouldn't have even come in today."

"You want to go home?"

Her response was instantaneous, "No!"

Gavril would be there, and he was the reason she felt she was coming apart at the seams. There was a part of her that wanted to abandon all reason and run headlong into his arms, but then there was the other part that was so terrified of him she wanted to run just as far and just as fast as she could. Only she feared that he could and would find her no matter where she fled.

Michael hooked a forefinger under her chin and made her face him. "Is there something going on besides the robbery, Mona? Has Darren been bothering you?"

"No… No… Shit! I don't know."

"You're in no shape to work."

"I don't want to go home, Michael."

"Why not?"

"I just don't. Let me stay. Please?"

"Mona, I care about you a hell of a lot. You know that. However, you are not in any shape to work in the office today. I can get Marie Jenkins, the mail girl, to drop her rounds and fill in for you. That sound okay? If you really don't want to go home, you can go down to the basement and go over the Tim Brown file again with a fine tooth comb for me. Guess I should have kept it out, but I put it back. That is, if you think you are up to it?"

"I can do it."

"You're sure?"

"Yes."

"Ok. See if anything in there strikes you as overlooked or unusual, anything we might use at all with the Harrison case."

"Yes. I can do that."

"You're sure?" he asked, reaching over and grabbing a tissue from the box on her desk. "Here."

"Thank you," she replied, finally able to smile faintly. She dabbed her eyes and tossed the tissue in the black trash can by her desk.

"That's better. I have to be in court in half an hour, but have lunch with me later. Okay? I'll call you when I'm done."

"Okay. Thank you!"

He kissed her forehead and left her to freshen up. She hurried to her desk and pulled out her compact. She had worn a black turtleneck sweater, not so much for the color but to cover her wound, the wound Gavril had inflicted upon her. She opened the compact up and gingerly pulled the sweater down to look. She'd put a large band aid over her wound, but it barely covered the two clean holes he had put there. She stared for a moment, having to convince herself that it was really there. Gavril was really a vampire and he had drunk blood from her. She snapped the compact shut, tossed it in her purse, and placed her purse in her desk drawer. Doing her best to put it all out of her mind and put on a courageous face, she said to herself, "Time to get it together, Mona. Time to get to work."

Gavril knew exactly what Mona was going through. She was having a very similar reaction to her profound knew knowledge that everyone else he'd ever transitioned went through. He was very aware of his ability to be irresistible; something he was capable of using on men as well as women. However, he preferred women and had turned only one man in his five-hundred-plus years. He could lure in the young as well as the old. His abilities held no bounds when it came to charming others, whether it was to merely feed from them or to turn them.

Mona was scared, which was perfectly normal and not unexpected. He didn't really want her afraid of him, but there was no way for her to escape the un-pleasantries that she was now destined for. It wasn't that he wanted to frighten her so much with the dreams, but she did need to fully fathom what would soon be her roots as well as his, for all vampires were connected in that sense, for they were neither dead nor alive. They were the undead, existing among the living.

The main hard fact was, in order to exist, they had to feed off of the living, and a sweet soul such as Mona would have great difficulty in dealing with that reality. It occurred to him that it was selfish of him to want to turn a young woman with such a gentle heart as hers, but his desire for a mate, his desire for her, was much more profound than any moral sense he might still harbor. No. He wanted her and had made up his mind to have her.

Right now, she was undergoing some internal, physical changes, but it was only the beginning of her transitioning. He had only fed her his blood once, and only a little. Some vampires would have fed her a great deal of blood and then killed her immediately, and she would have awoken with horrible cravings and not understanding at all what was happening. He'd always considered that method cold and harsh, remembering his own turning. Dracula had not been caring, to say the least. Gavril had gone through hell. Once he got his cravings under control and understood his true nature, he vowed to never do what his sire had done to him. In fact, when he finally had the opportunity, he surprised his sire and killed him, and not just for the way he had turned him, but for revenge for killing the woman he loved.

Over the years there had been countless tales, different versions, of the way the famous vampire had met his demise. However, only Gavril and the few he had chosen to share his story with knew the truth. What's more, he really didn't care. He was free of his cousin and had gotten his revenge. That was all that mattered to him.

He would turn Mona slowly. It would also give her time to think about what was happening to her, and he hoped that the end result would be that she would want to be turned. That was what he would strive for, but it wasn't something he could rush into. Also, after all was said and done, if he saw that she truly did not want to join him in the ranks of the undead, he could quit giving her his blood, let her heal for a few days and then hypnotize her to forget all that had happened, and he would just disappear. Most vampires would just kill their subject, but not Gavril. Although he was deadly and powerful, there was still a semblance of humanity left in him, at least for those he cared about, human or vampire. That he did not want to ever lose.

Darren stuck his head into his dad's office.

Michael glanced up. "What, Darren?"

"You have plans for lunch?"

That got Michael's attention. He leaned back in his chair. "What's up? But to answer your question: No. I had a luncheon planned with Mona, but she's kind of out of it, so I said we could do it tomorrow."

"That's what I want to talk to you about… Mona."

It was clear on Michael's face that he thought Darren was up to something. "If you're worried about Mona and me, we're not actually dating. Not right now, anyway."

"It's not that, Dad. I swear. I'm worried about her."

"Seriously?" There was something in Darren's eyes that said he was on the up and up. "Okay." He glanced at his watch. "How about now?"

Looking through her open door, Darren noticed Mona wasn't in her office. "Did you send her home?"

"She didn't want to go home, but she's working on some files in the basement."

Darren flinched slightly, but he didn't address it. "Now is good for lunch. Thanks, Dad."

"Okay. Let me send Mona a text, and then we can go. See if she wants us to bring her back something."

"All right, I'll wait for you by the watercooler."

Mona's phone beeped and she glanced at her message. Michael was going to lunch with Darren. "That's a new one," she mumbled to herself, and quickly texted back that he could bring her a ham sandwich, and stuck her phone back in the side pocket of her dark green pantsuit that she had chosen to go with the black sweater. It seemed to her that she'd already gone through Tim Brown's file at least a half dozen times, but she picked it up and thumbed through it again. That was when something caught her eye. Something that she could not believe she had missed before. The young girl that Brown was convicted of raping, Trisha Landsbury, mentioned something about a birthmark on her rapist's chest. There was no other mention of it though in any of the court documents that Mona could remember. "That's strange. Was there no mention of it in the trial?" She wasn't sure why at that moment, but for some reason that really bothered her. Surely something like a birthmark would have come out. Did Tim Brown have a birthmark on his chest? She set the file aside, which was separate from the court documents, as the case had been turned over to another law firm.

She contemplated a minute. "Hmmm…" A thought came to her. "I wonder… Does Rick Harrison have a birthmark on his chest?" She hurriedly put the files back in the cabinet. Michael was at lunch and wouldn't need her for a while. Besides, Marie was filling in for her today. Before hurrying off to the elevator, she would just grab her purse and head straight to the county jail.

Harrison glanced up from the long black table where he was sitting, surprised but glad to see Mona. "I was half expecting Michael Graves to come in today, but not you. A pleasant surprise."

"Michael doesn't even know I'm here. I just came across something in a file on a different rape case that took place five years ago."

"What could an old case have to do with mine?"

"Maybe nothing… Maybe everything. I need to know. Do you have a birthmark of any kind on your chest?"

"Huh?" he said, taken aback by her question. "No! I don't have any birthmarks…anywhere."

"It's not that I don't believe you, but could you show me your chest?"

"Ok, I guess," he replied and unzipped the top of his orange uniform and pulled up his Tee-shirt so she could see. "No birthmarks." Just a very well-sculptured chest met her eyes, but no birthmarks, no blemishes of any kind. It was apparent that he kept in shape.

"Great. Thank you!" she said, thinking he was kind of hot, but no comparison to Gavril. She shuddered.

"You okay?" he asked.

"Yes… Just a little chill." It was true. Simply thinking of Gavril made her quiver all over.

"It is kind of cool in here." He pulled his Tee-shirt back down and zipped his uniform up. "I hope the fact that I don't have any birthmarks will help."

"At this time, I can't promise anything, Rick, but let's hope so." She stood. "Thank you! You've been very helpful."

"Not a problem. Thank you for your efforts."

Nodding slightly, she left.

Mona knew that she might have to pay Tim Brown a visit too, but she needed to find out if the subject of a birthmark had been brought up during his trial.

At first, Shane Williams thought that Michael Graves had sent Mona over to see him about Margaret. "This is a bit of a surprise," he said to the pretty honey blonde. With an outstretched hand, he indicated to the two black leather chairs in front of his desk. "Take your pick."

She chose the one to the right. "Thank you for seeing me on such a short notice. But I need to know something about an old case. Didn't you defend Tim Brown in that rape case five years ago?"

He was obviously surprised. "Yes I did. Not one of my more successful cases. Why?"

"I was going through some old files in the basement, and I noticed something that I don't remember being brought up in court. At least, I don't recall hearing anything about it."

"What is that?"

"In the file we have, one Michael started when he was considering taking on the case, before he turned it over to you, the rape victim claimed Tim had a birthmark on his chest. Only, I can't find any reference to it anywhere else."

"Oh! Yeah... The alleged birthmark. She was pretty adamant about it, but there wasn't one." He kind of laughed and leaned back in his chair and tossed a pencil he'd been holding to his desk. "Come to find out, she must have scratched Tim when she was trying to fight him off and in her hysterical state thought it was a birthmark. All the other evidence fit perfectly. There was a roundish scratch. He claimed he got it when he was working on his car. It had healed, though, by the time the case went to court."

"Oh! So he doesn't have a birthmark?"

"Nope. Not a one."

She inhaled deeply and exhaled. "Okay. That answers my question. I just wondered why no more was said of it."

"There was… in court. But it was established that she just confused the scratch with a birthmark. It could have easily been construed as a birthmark by a hysterical young woman."

"Okay. That's all I needed to know." She stood.

"Anything else I can help you with?"

"No. You've been very helpful. Thank you!"

"Anytime."

Walking out, heading for her car, she tossed everything over and over in her mind. Tim Brown had sat in prison for five years for a rape she did not believe he committed, and now the same fate might be awaiting Rick Harrison. Neither man had a birthmark on his chest, but she knew someone who did – Darren! The coincidence was so uncanny. She didn't want to believe it, but something told her that this nagging feeling she had was right. All three men were blond with similar builds and hazel eyes. Only one had a birthmark on his chest. "Oh dear God! What do I do now?" She knew that something like this would really hurt Michael in more ways than one. He was a wonderful man with a great career, but something of this magnitude leaking out could destroy the firm, which, in turn, would destroy him. That she did not want to happen. Still, could she let two innocent men (one already having lost five years of his life) pay for crimes they had not committed? Now, she had no doubts that that was what Darren had wanted the file for. He had wanted to see if the incriminating evidence was still there. It hit her then that she needed to get back and put the file someplace where Darren couldn't find it. She couldn't get back to the firm fast enough.

Michael found it hard to believe, at first, that Darren really thought Mona was in danger from this new tenant in her building. "You sure you're not just jealous, Darren?" he said as he peered over his glass of iced tea.

"I know I'm an ass a lot of the time, Dad. What's more, I admit that I really screwed up ditching Mona for Nancy, and Mona doesn't want me back. It hurts, but it is what I deserve. However, you've got to believe me. There is something really wrong about this Count Conta or whatever his name is."

Michael sat his tea down. "According to the news, the man is something of a hero, Darren. He stopped a robbery last night. Possibly saved your former landlady from what could have been serious injuries... or worse."

"I know. I saw all that on the news. Still, Dad, he scares the living crap out of me. I've never felt such... such... evil! Yes! Evil is the word I'm looking for. He gives me the willies like no one ever has before."

Michael noticed his son's hands trembling as he tried to eat the salad in front of him. He sat his fork down. "Okay, Darren. I see this has you really upset. What do you want me to do?"

"I know this is going to be a little weird, even awkward, with the given situation, but Mona won't have anything to do with me. Still, I need to know that she is okay. Can you keep an eye on her for me? Please?"

"I can try, Son. I thought it wise to back off from seeing her because I could see she likes this guy. However, if you truly believe she is in danger from him, I will make an effort to gain her attentions again."

"Thank you, Dad! That's all I ask. Thank you!"

"Of course, Son." Michael understood now that his son really had true feelings for Mona. It was a shame that he had realized it too late. "I can't promise anything. But I will do what I can to look after her."

The waitress brought their check. "I'll get this, Dad."

"You sure?" Michael had to ask, for always in the past Darren seemed to expect his father to pick up the tab, no matter where they went. Michael knew it was his fault, though. He and Margaret were both guilty of spoiling him.

"I want to get it."
"Fine by me."
Finished with their lunch, they returned to the office.

Chapter Six:

Darren and Michael arrived at the office shortly after Mona. Marie had been at Mona's desk when she came back up and told her that the two had gone to lunch together.

"I know. They're bringing me a sandwich."

"Are you feeling better now?" Marie asked.

"Yes! Yes I am. In fact, if you want, you can go to lunch." She was feeling much better. Having something as important to focus on in believing Darren might be guilty, had helped free her mind of the previous night, even though she didn't want to be right.

"You're sure?"

"Absolutely. And thanks."

"You're welcome," the little brunette smiled behind her glasses and walked out, leaving Mona to her desk.

Michael walked in just as Marie was leaving. Mona could see Darren through the glass to the outer office. He was eyeing her inquisitively. She smiled vaguely, not wanting him to suspect anything, and he reflected her smile and walked off.

"You're looking a lot better," Michael noted as he stepped just inside the door.

"I'm okay now. I let Marie go to lunch."

"I see that. Great." He paused briefly, considering something, and then he asked, "Would you have dinner with me again... tonight?"

Instantly, she thought about Gavril – *He wanted her to be his mate!* Though she wanted him too, desired him more than anything, the thought still terrified her. "Yes!" she practically blurted. "Yes! I'll have dinner with you."

Tickled by this unexpected response from her – had anticipated a no – his face lit up like Christmas. "Awesome! I'll pick you up at seven. That give you enough time to get ready?"

"Plenty... And, you have a Mr. Lund waiting to see you."

"Send him in." He winked happily and returned to his desk.

Gavril knew right away that Mona was resisting him, resisting him fiercely now; fear of the unknown still overriding desire. It wasn't unexpected, and he was not disappointed. He didn't want her sleeping with Michael though, wanted her for himself. There was certainly the possibility that she would willingly go to bed with the man in order to cling to the humanity she was comfortable with and afraid of losing. It was also not his desire to harm Michael, but he could and would make attempting a relationship with Mona most difficult for him, to say the least.

Gavril remained in his apartment when Mona hurried in from work. He knew she was going to dinner with Michael – That was allowed. However, later, should they try to become a little more intimate, then he would intervene. There was no doubt that they would come back to her apartment, for Michael would not take Mona home where his wife still lived.

Michael took Mona to Roberto's, a fine new Italian restaurant, where the lights were low and soft romantic music filtered in through hidden speakers. After his earlier discussion with Darren, he had decided to just go for it. So what, if he was older than Mona, she was attracted to him and liked him, and he more than wanted her. He would do anything to protect this lovely young woman sitting across from him, smiling so beautifully. Anything! Even if it meant giving up his own life for her, he wouldn't hesitate. In spite of her smile, she did seem a little distracted. He wondered if Gavril was on her mind. He felt it unwise to broach the subject at that particular moment, though.

It was she who finally broke the mundane pleasantries by asking, "What made you change your mind?"

"Change my mind? Oh! You mean about asking you out?"

"Yes. I remember that I was told, and quite distinctly, that you wanted to give me more time."

He smiled apologetically. "That's correct. At first, but then I decided that I agreed with the old adage, 'all is fair in love and war.'"

That brought on an even bigger smile. "Sounds fair enough."

"To change the subject, Mona…"

She sat her iced tea glass down. "What?"

"You don't have any problems with your new neighbor, do you?"

The question caught her completely off her guard. She'd been trying so hard not to think about Gavril, and the almost overwhelming, and oh-so-lustful desire he invoked in her. It was damn near impossible to endure. She wanted him, vampire or not, to take her in his arms and do unspeakable, erotic things to her. A warm surge flushed her face. "Uh…" She coughed and took a quick sip of her tea, looking away momentarily to gain her composure. After a few seconds, she sat the glass aside, took a deep breath and faced Michael again. "He's somewhat of a hero, you know.'

Her reaction did not go unnoticed by Michael, but he did not address it. "So I heard. Saw it on the news. However, that doesn't answer my question, Mona. Does he frighten you in any way?"

Now she was feeling strangely defensive for Gavril. Her brow instantly furrowed and she replied, "Why would you ask that?" She thought about it then. "Darren! Darren said something to you, didn't he?"

"Please, Mona. Not my intention to upset you. But yes. Darren has concerns about the man. Says the man gives him the creeps."

"Seriously?" Voice suddenly strained.

Michael could readily see that the subject was upsetting her, but she was trying hard not to show it. "I'm sorry. Not my intention to spoil our evening. I wanted it to be… special."

She cocked her head slightly sideways. "Is that why you changed your mind about asking me out again?"

She had him. Silently, he sat there trying to figure out how to respond, knowing this was not going over well. "I want to be with you, Mona. I really do."

"But you asked me out because of what Darren said, didn't you?"

He took hold of her hand. "I like you a lot. You've got to know that. I want to be with you, more than anything in this world. Nevertheless, to answer your question – Yes! I figured that if Darren is afraid for you, then I want to make absolutely sure that you are okay."

She withdrew her hand from his and leaned back in her seat, disappointment replacing any semblance of a smile. "I don't need a babysitter, Michael. I need a friend." She picked up her black clutch purse. "I'm sorry. This is all lovely and everything…" she made a sweeping gesture with her arm, "but I am *not* in the mood anymore. Would you please take me home?"

"I'm sorry, Mona. Please! I wanted this to be a lovely evening."

"So did I." She stood.

He blew out air. She'd made up her mind. He'd screwed up big time.

"Let's take Mona home, Charlie," Michael said to his chauffeur, as he held the door open for them.

"All right, sir."

Michael wanted to talk with Mona more, get the air cleared, but she just wasn't open for discussing it. After a couple of attempts, he left her alone. When they reached her apartment, Mona insisted on going in alone. The lights in the drugstore were still on. It wasn't late, so Michael didn't argue.

As Charlie held the door open for her to get out, Michael said, "I'm sorry, Mona. But to risk sounding like a stuck recording – I did want to be with you this evening."

She nodded, but didn't say anything, turned and headed for the front door. Charlie stood by the car and watched until she was inside, then he got in.

"Just take me home, Charlie."

"Right, sir." He glanced at his boss in the rearview again. "I'm sorry your date didn't turn out so well, sir."

"Me too. Thanks."

"Perhaps next time it will be better, sir."

"Perhaps." He had a gut–feeling there wouldn't be a next time.

Charlie dropped the car in gear and they drove off.

Gavril was not unhappy that Michael had apparently blown it. He sensed Mona's emotional turmoil before she ever stepped out of the limousine. She had been searching for emotional support from Michael. Instead, she felt as though she were being watched over like a helpless child. That was part of the problem; she felt helpless, needed Michael for emotional backing, not feel like he was a parent figure guarding over her.

Mona barely burst into her apartment before she threw her small purse as hard as she could across the kitchen. She stood there growling like an enraged animal. "Dammit!" she screeched, slamming the door closed. Her kitchen window rattled. "Dammit!" There was an empty glass sitting by the sink. She snatched it up and threw it against the wall, shattering it into tiny shards that flew everywhere. She burst out sobbing, all the while, grabbing the broom and dustpan out of the tiny closet in the corner of the kitchen and attempting to sweep up the tiny pieces. At one point, she pricked her finger and it began to bleed. She stuck her finger in her mouth to suck the blood off.

She stopped.

She removed her finger and stared. More blood seeped out. She sucked it off too and withdrew her finger. "What the *hell?*" She stood there staring at the blood still leaking out of her finger and spilling down across her knuckle. It struck her that she was hungry, but not for food – She hungered for blood! "Oh my God! What is wrong with me?" Sniffling again, she rushed over to the sink and ran water over her finger, washing away the blood that refused to stop oozing.

She never felt so unglued and out of control. She laughed and then she cried and then she laughed some more. She felt she was losing her mind.

Then there was a soft knock on her door. "Mona?"

It was Gavril. The very person she didn't want to see, and yet, did. She shut the water off and stepped back, standing at the threshold of her small living room, staring at the door. Did she dare open it? Did she dare let in the man that had done this do her? What made it worse was in simply hearing his voice, her breast swelled and felt all warm. She suddenly wanted to spread her legs for him. "Shit! What's wrong with me?"

"Mona, I know you're in there. I know you're upset. Please let me in."

"Go away! I'm okay. Go away!" But she wasn't. She wanted him! Oh how she wanted him. She was vibrating from her intense desire and need for him.

"You're not okay. I can hear you very clearly. You're crying."

"Shit!" she hissed between her teeth. She stared at the shards of glass all over her kitchen floor. "I broke a glass. Need to sweep it up. Don't want to step on any glass and get a cut when I'm running around barefoot." She held up her finger. It seemed to have ceased bleeding.

"I am not worried about a little broken glass, Mona. Let me in and I'll help you clean it up."

"Oh! What the hell!" She unlocked the door and opened it. She gasped as she beheld his handsome face. More handsome than she remembered. Was that possible? "Come in." She furiously fought her desire to wrap her arms around him and beg him to take her right then and there. Instead, she quietly stepped aside and let him walk in.

She closed the door.

Gavril surveyed the mess. "Don't worry, my sweet. I'll have it cleaned up for you in no time." He picked up the broom and dustpan, and then he was a blur, moving so fast she could barely tell it was him. Seconds later, he stopped. The glass was all cleaned up, and he returned the dustpan and broom to her closet. He faced her, smiling his wonderful, mysterious smile. "Is that better?"

She nodded yes.

He zipped up to her, no longer hiding his true vampire self in her presence.

She stared up into those amazing black depths that twinkled with little lights. "Better… Yes. Thank you!" Something came over her. Something she couldn't explain. An incredible warm surge made its way through her entire being as she gazed, hypnotized into his dark eyes. *Take me now! Please! Have your way with me!*

"So glad you are feeling better."

Breathlessly, she asked, "What have you done to me?"

This apparently amused him. "I let you sample my blood."

"I feel so unglued. I don't like feeling this way – out of control."

He slipped an arm around her waist and led her to her sofa, where they sat down. "You're just scared. You're fighting it. Stop fighting it and you'll be okay."

She wasn't certain what was worse – the fear or the insane need for him to make love to her. If he were picking up her thoughts, though, he wasn't addressing it. "I am scared, Gavril. I don't know what to expect. I'm freakin' terrified!" *Not to mention horny beyond belief!*

"Of how you feel? Or of what you think you might become?"

She glanced off to the side and then back to him. "I haven't thought about it. I just know I'm scared." *And I want you to fuck me. Oh yes! Please, please fuck me!*

"Think it over. Run it over in that pretty head of yours. What are you really afraid of?"

"Of becoming a vampire. Until a short time ago, I believed vampires to be a myth. I had no clue they could be real." She crossed her left leg over her right. She was wet, wetter in hell between her legs. *Shit!*

"It is a little frightening in the beginning. The blood cravings are overwhelming in the beginning. In fact, if you think you like the taste of blood now, just wait until you transition."

"You're freakin' kidding me. I hope!" *Gads! Ravage me… please!*

"I would never kid you about something so serious as transitioning, Mona."

There was a short pause while she studied his eyes, his expression, and his amazing composure. "I've never met anyone so… so sure of themselves. Do you ever get rattled?"

"I have seen much in my long life, Mona. There is very little that rattles me."

"You keep saying long life. Just how long? You don't look a day over thirty-five. How old are you?" *Jeeze! I couldn't be any wetter!*

"You're only off about five hundred years."

"Five hundred—." Mouth gaping, she shook her head, unbelieving. *"Five hundred years?"*

"Actually a few more than that, going on six hundred now. Yet, I've known vampires much older than I. Not many, though."

"You are freakin' kiddin' me?"

"My sire's sire was over a thousand years old."

"Your what?" *I can't stand it! Take me!*

"My sire's sire. That is what one calls the vampire that turns them – their sire. If I turn you," a smile grew across his face, "I will be your sire."

"You're still intent on turning me?"

An eyebrow rose. "Are you really so opposed to the idea?" He was very aware of how much she wanted to be with him, how hard she was fighting off the powerful urge to simply succumb to his will, but she was weakening, weakening fast.

She turned her face to the side, afraid to look into those beckoning, obsidian caverns anymore. *If you don't fuck me right now, I am going to lose my freakin' mind.*

He gently reached over and turned her face back to his. "I want you, Mona. I want to take you to bed and make love to you. Would you be willing to let me do that? Right now?"

It was all she could do not to scream out yes. The warmth she was feeling in her breasts simply being under his stare, the mad craving that was making itself known internally could not be ignored. Every sinew within her wanted him to make love to her. She sprang up and ran to the kitchen, only to find him standing before her. "Shit!" There was no way she was going to escape him now, even if she wanted to, and she didn't.

He knew this. It was his power. It was obvious in his smile. He kissed her. She let out a little gasp as he placed his hands on her buttocks and pressed her into him. Even though she really didn't want to, she made a feeble attempt to fight him off, but then submitted, returning his kiss, realizing she was vibrating herself up against him.

Laughing lighting, knowing full well what he was doing to her, he swiftly swept her into his arms and carried her to bed. In mere seconds, he removed her clothes as well as his own. His lips found hers again, and in the middle of the most wonderful kiss he claimed her. "Oh shit!" she breathed, instantly responding, giving in to him in total surrender.

She was on fire. Sweet, wonderful, all-consuming fire blazed through her whole being, as she gave herself to him wholly. She'd never known such ecstasy, such wanton desire. There was a second of pain as he bit into her neck and she knew he was feeding from her again, but she was so enraptured by his love-making that she did not care. She was his. She no longer had a will of her own. Her insides burned with the rapturous craving, the all-consuming need for him. He owned her completely and totally. Even though she felt herself growing weaker as he drank her blood, she clung to him, wrapping her legs around him, not wanting him to ever let her go. Then, just as she experienced the most wickedly wonderful climax, he exploded into her. She cried out, "Oh damn yes!" as they fused together in complete bliss.

He held her firmly until their passion began to subside. His black eyes beheld hers. "You're weak my sweet, time for me to feed you." He ripped open his wrist and placed it over her mouth, where she drank eagerly. "There... There... my sweet. Drink heartily. It will give you strength."

She did. She eagerly took in his life-giving nourishment. Feeling his amazing power surge through her whole being. Then he pulled his wrist away. Once more, it closed up immediately.

"Enough, my darling. Enough for now. How do you feel?"

"A little weak, but okay."

"Good. I've drained you of a lot of your blood. Mine will give you sufficient strength to get through the day tomorrow, but you will tire easily. In fact, you might want to stay home?"

"No. I can't do that. Michael is swamped with clients and court appearances. I can't abandon him now.

"As you wish, my sweet, but you may have to cut your day short." Noting her disappointed expression, he added, "But then you may feel just fine." He changed the subject. "You know… You belong to me now?"

Eyes glued to his, she replied, "Yes."

"It will be forever. I will ask you this once and only once. This is your chance to say no. Do you wish to back out?"

She considered his question. He was so awesome, so mesmerizing. There was no way she could picture herself ever being with another man after being with him. "…No."

"You will accompany me then, and ride with me on the back of forever?"

"Yes! Forever!"

Pleased with her response, he kissed her sweetly and then released her, rolling off and pulling the covers up over them both. He laid an arm across her chest and peered down at her. "I must inform you that it is going to get a little harder before we're done."

"What do you mean?"

"Right now, you have cravings…"

"Tell me about it," she hotly breathed.

He chuckled naughtily. "Not just sex, my dear. I was referring to the craving for blood, and you will experience some of what it is like to be a vampire. However, you are not a vampire yet. You are going to get much sicker before we are done. Much, much sicker."

"…What?"

"Have you ever watched any of the old vampire movies?"

"Yes. When I was a kid."

"Keep in mind that all fiction is based on some truths."

"I suppose it is."

"Then you must know that in order to fully transition you must die first."

She gulped and stared up into his amazing eyes. "I guess I kind of knew that. Just didn't want to think about it."

"Your last few days will be difficult, to say the least. But not to worry. Once you die, it won't be long before you arise and will be like me, a vampire."

"When?"

"The next time I feed you my blood should do it." He smiled strangely then, as though something amused him. "Or… it could be sooner."

"I appreciate you telling me… I think."

Another chuckle accompanied with a wink. He was suddenly out of bed and dressed before she could even get up. He handed over her clothes and assisted her in dressing.

"Will it hurt?" she asked, as he finished zipping up her pants for her. "Will I suffer much?"

"I won't lie. It won't be pleasant."

She sighed and offered him a faint smile. She was feeling kind of out of it.

"Trying to be brave. I admire that." He kissed her forehead. "Now don't worry your pretty little head about it… Did you finish your dinner with Michael?"

"Not really."

"Are you hungry? For human food, that is?"

"I could eat some more."

"I just happen to have a couple of T-bones in my refrigerator. Why don't you come on across to my place while I cook dinner for us?"

"Cool. I never thought of you as a cook before."

"After five hundred years, Mona? Don't you think I might have mastered the art of cooking, along with a few other things, in all that time?"

"I suppose you would be very good at many things."

"I am. Trust me."

Her eyes crinkled in a smile. "Oh I do! Or I wouldn't be—. " She didn't finish. He understood fully what she wanted to relay.

There was another warm chuckle, as he hung an arm around her shoulder and escorted her to his apartment.

Margaret stood from the sofa, looking elegant as ever in her silk, red lounging pajamas. She'd been watching her husband ever since he'd come in. He was not himself. "What is it, Michael?" she said, moving over to their little bar and taking a stool. "Something went wrong with your dinner date with Mona, didn't it?"

He sat the bottle of whiskey down and stirred his drink. "You asking because you care? Or so you can relish in my pain?"

"Mix me one of those, would you?"

He nodded.

"I don't deny that we don't have what we used to, Michael. And I don't deny that I can be and have been a total bitch at times."

That got his attention. His brow wrinkled marginally. "What are you saying, Margaret?" He handed over her drink.

"In spite of it all, Michael, believe it or not, I do care about your wellbeing."

"Really… " His snicker was faint but audible.

"I'm serious, Michael. Shane was kind of a last straw with me. I think I was hoping to find something new in him. But nothing. Nada. He is just as self-centered, shallow and egotistical as the rest of us."

"Speak for yourself. I know I'm not what I ought to be, but I am working on it."

"I can see that. I've seen you changing. And to tell you the truth, I kind of hoped things wouldn't work out between you and Mona."

"Seriously?" He walked around and took a stool by her.

"Seriously. I have to admit that I kind of like to see this… this new you. It's kind of refreshing."

"You're not just saying that because things didn't work out with you and Shane?"

"Ouch!" she said and took a sip of her drink before setting the glass aside. "I deserved that. So, I won't hold it against you. I couldn't be more serious, Michael."

"Are you trying to tell me now, after all this time, and all the crap we've dealt out to one another that you want to give us a try?"

"I don't know. Maybe that is what I'm trying to say." Her eyes dilated slightly. She was telling the truth.

He took a slow sip of his drink, considering what his wife was saying. "I have to tell you, I'm not sure where I am at right now. If you are really sincere, give me time to think about it. Is that all right with you?"

"Fair enough." She lit a cigarette and blew the smoke to the side, away from him.

"Well, I have to admit, I never believed we'd be having this conversation. Maybe there is hope for us after all." He finished off his drink and stood. "I'm going to take a shower."

She nodded and finished off her own drink and went around for a refill.

Mona had grown very tired right after dinner with Gavril, and had gone to bed soon as she returned to her apartment and fell into a deep sleep. When she awoke the next morning, she couldn't remember dreaming at all. For that, she was kind of grateful, for she had slept well, had slept hard. It was something she needed, but when she went to the bathroom to brush her teeth, she jumped back in horror at the reflection peering back at her. Dark circles under her eyes and her skin was chalky white. She felt like crap, which Gavril had warned her about. But this! "Oh dear God!" Tentatively, she touched her fingers to her face, realizing her hands were ice cold. "Shit!" Panic seized her and her heart went into high gear.

Across the hall, Gavril knew immediately that Mona was up and experiencing the harsh reality of what was happening to her. It was something she had to go through, and it would be hard, but she could do it. He had given her the option of backing out, something he'd never done before. He only did it because she was so young and he really did care about her. He also knew she was about to knock on his door and had it open before her closed fist met the wood. "Good morning, my sweet," he said, laying a gentle hand on her shoulder and helping her inside.

Facing him, she said, "I can't go to work like this! I look like death warmed over."

He chuckled amusedly.

"Why are you laughing? This is serious!"

"I know, my dear. However, that is just it. You *are* death warmed over."

"Huh?"

"You are close to death as a human, but even closer to immortality as a vampire. My blood in you is the only thing making it possible for you to be standing. Therefore, you are sort of death warmed over. I did not mean to be insensitive to your plight."

"I knew I'd be sick. Still, I didn't expect to look like this!"

"Makeup, my sweet. Haven't you some makeup you can wear to hide the dark circles? To hide the paleness of your skin?"

"What about my arms and hands?"

"Long sleeves, perhaps? But gloves would probably just bring on unwanted attention."

Momentarily, she glanced down at the floor, thinking over his suggestions, and then faced him again. "Long sleeves aren't a problem. It's cool outside. And I do have makeup base. I don't wear it most of the time, but I do have some."

"I strongly suggest you apply it. Or else, stay home."

"Not an option. Not today. Michael needs me in court with him."

"Your choice. However, need I remind you that at some point – very soon, I might add – you are going to have to leave your job?"

"What?" Her brow narrowed. She hadn't even thought that one through. "Oh my gosh! You're right. When I'm a vampire, I won't be able to go out in the sunlight, will I?"

"Definitely not. However, on really cloudy, overcast days, you can sometimes venture out for a short time. I don't recommend it though. One never knows when the sun might decide to pop out again. And then you'd be in serious trouble. One tends to blister really fast. Instantaneous, as a matter of fact." He snorted cynically. "Actually, I think the first case of spontaneous combustion was actually an ill-informed, new vampire."

"Oh my God!" She inhaled and held it briefly before letting it out in a long sigh. "Okay. Ah... I really need to think all this through."

"Yes, my dear. You need to prepare for your future life in the ranks of the undead. You need to get on it right away."

"Okay." She gazed up into his seemingly bottomless black depths that served as his eyes. "I thought I knew what I was doing, but guess I didn't fully fathom all of it." As weak as she was, as she stared up into his handsome face, she realized she wanted him as much as ever. She had a feeling that the need she felt for him wasn't going to go away. At least, not any time soon.

"One never does, as you say, 'fathom all of it'. A common mistake for a transitioning vampire. It takes a while to fully grasp the profound alterations in ones ways of... living."

"I'm beginning to see that." Her expression changed markedly.

"You're wondering if it is too late to change your mind, aren't you?"

After a brief hesitation, she nodded yes.

"I asked you last night."

Tears came to her eyes. "I know. It's too late, isn't it?"

This was not totally unexpected. He took her face between his palms and stared deep into her eyes. "I have never done this before, Mona. Therefore, consider yourself *very* special. I will let you think about today."

She gasped happily.

"Only today, though. You will have to make your final decision before midnight."

"Oh thank you! Thank you!"

He wiped a tear off her cheek with his thumb. "Now quit crying and go put on some makeup and go to work. Spend your day as normally as you can, and while you do, compare your life as a human and that of what being a vampire and living forever could be. Tonight, I will come see you for your decision."

"Thank you!" she said again and hugged him as enthusiastically as her weakened state would allow.

"Have a good day, my sweet."

She put on a courageous smile and walked out the door.

"I must be softening in my old age," Gavril said to himself. "I have never softened like that before. I guess the young lady means more to me than I realized. Perhaps it is because she reminds me so much of Alina." He decided it was time to make himself a tall drink.

"I screwed up," Michael told his son who appeared in his office doorway.

Incredulous, Darren asked, "How? Mona likes you. How did you screw up?" He squeezed the bridge of his nose with his thumb and forefinger and then dropped his hand down.

Michael told him briefly how his ill-fated conversation had quickly gone south during his dinner date with Mona the night before.

Shaking his head, he said, "That's a new one. I can see myself making a mistake like that, but not you, Dad."

"Circumstances completely caught me off my guard. Goes to show we can't always be right. Or perfect." As an afterthought, he added, "Definitely not perfect."

Both did a double-take as Mona breezed in past them in a gray pantsuit and into her office, barely uttering a good morning, but looking white as a ghost. Father and son exchanged glances. Michael shrugged and Darren mouthed, "She looks horrible!"

With an agreeing nod, Michael jumped up from his desk and went in to see about Mona. Darren remained at the door.

Mona turned around. "What?"

"I never thought I'd say this to you, but you look like crap! You sure you want to be here?"

"Something I ate last night, Michael. I'll be okay." She sat down to her desk.

"Maybe you should have stayed and had your dinner with me."

"Maybe. Maybe not." She made herself busy, shuffling some papers around, not really looking at him.

Michael glanced back and Darren and signaled for him to go on. Darren nodded and disappeared.

"I can have Marie come back, if you're ill? I don't want you working, if you're not up to it." Just then, rising from her chair, she moved in such a way that he noticed a rather large band aid low on her neck just under her collar. "You cut yourself?"

"What?" She jerked her head up.

"Your neck, Mona. That's a big band aid. I know you don't shave. What happened?"

She didn't reply right away. Stood there silently, pondering and looked off.

"Mona, I am truly sorry about last evening. Also, I can live with the fact that you're not happy with me right now, but something doesn't feel right here. I care about you, Mona!"

The resonance in his voice made her face him again. "I'm sorry," she replied apologetically, expression softening. "I care about you too. I just have some personal matters on my mind."

"You know you can tell me anything, don't you?"

Observing him thoughtfully, she replied, "I know. This is something I have to work out for myself, though. You can't really help me with it."

He was a little hurt, but said he understood.

She quickly added, "You do mean a lot to me, Michael, but I have to be honest with you."

"Oh? I'm not so sure I'm going to like what's coming."

"There's someone else I have feelings for. Strong feelings."

"Count Conta, right?"

She nodded yes and said, "I'm sorry. I didn't really realize it until last night – That he was what was bothering me, I mean."

"I think I had an inkling." Definitely hurt now, he tried to hide it, but it showed in his eyes, and he grimaced marginally. "You didn't tell me what happened to your neck."

"Oh! That… Well, I managed to scrape it. Was bending over in my closet and didn't realize there was a wire hanger askew. When I went to rise up, the damn thing got me. Got me pretty good."

"Did you go to the emergency room?"

"No. It's not that bad. I got the bleeding stopped and got an antibiotic from Harry." That part was true. She had told Harry the very same story that morning before she came to work. She smiled faintly. "Leave it to me to cut myself on a clothes hanger, of all things."

"Looks like you had a rough evening all the way around. I'm sorry. Still, you let me know if you decide you aren't up to finishing up the day."

"I will. Promise."

"Okay." He glanced at his watch. "We're due in court in half an hour."

"I'm on it," she replied.

He disappeared into his office to prepare for court, but he was still uneasy about Mona. She looked awful.

Gavril was surprised at himself. He had stronger feelings for Mona than he had realized. He wanted her for a mate. Of that, there was no doubt. Always before, though, with any other woman he turned for a mate, once the decision had been made, he would not renege on it. The fact that he could care this much for a mere human had taken him aback more than a little. Definitely, he had amazed himself.

What would he do if she decided she didn't want to be turned? Instead of killing her, which many vampires would do, what he had done in the past, he would erase her memory and leave. She would never see him again, nor would she even remember him. He would not forget her, though. She would be ingrained in his memory forever, as the only woman he had ever loved, besides Alina, enough to set free. It wouldn't be easy, but for her, he would do it.

Darren was in court too, waiting to be heard on one of his own cases. He couldn't help but stare at Mona. Even though she put on a smile when looked at and was making a strong effort to act normal, he could tell she was very ill. His dad was fully aware of this too, but he kept indicating that Mona wanted to be there. There was nothing he could do.

On the way out of the courtroom, Michael stopped Mona. "You take a cab here?"

"Yes. Didn't want to drive my car. Feeling a bit unsteady."

"You ride back with me. In fact, let me take you home?"

"No!" she promptly replied without hesitation.

Brow furrowed, he said, "Are you afraid to go home?"

She stopped in her tracks just as they were exiting the building. "What do you mean by that?"

"The way you answered. I get the strong feeling that there is a reason you don't want to go home. I'll come out and say it. Is it Conta? Are you afraid of him?"

"Of course not," she replied, but she blinked nervously.

He knew her very well, and he'd been a lawyer long enough to hone the ability of detecting a lie. He didn't want to accuse her though. She was in no condition for him to put her through an interrogating argument. "All right then. Let me take you home. Later, Darren can follow me over in your car to bring it back. What do you say?"

She went to reply but suddenly felt faint.

He caught her in his arms. "That does it. I am taking you to the hospital."

"No!" she cried, hysteria rising.

"You're sick, Mona. You require medical attention. Something is very wrong."

"Food poisoning. I'll get over it. Just need to rest. No hospital!"

"Okay," he replied in as calming a tone as possible. "But I'm taking you home right now!" He scooped her up in his arms and carried her down the steps and to his car, wishing he'd had his

127/Back of Forever: Vampire Mine/Waldron

chauffeur, but he mostly used Charlie and the limousine for social functions.

Mona fell asleep on the way home. Michael saw a place to pull over and texted Darren that he was taking Mona home; she had passed out, to have Marie take over for Mona the rest of the day. Darren texted back immediately that he was on it, just take care of Mona.

When Matilda caught sight of Michael carrying Mona in the front door, she forgot about the perfume display and rushed over. "Dear Lord! What's wrong?" she anxiously asked Michael, for Mona looked not only pale as a sheet but out of it.

"Says it was food poisoning."

"She should see a doctor!"

"I know. She got hysterical when I suggested it."

Harry saw too, but he was waiting on a customer in the drug department. "I have something I can give her to sooth her stomach," he said. "I'll be up in a minute with it."

"Good!" Michael replied, heading through the door to the stairwell with Matilda at his feet.

Gavril was keenly aware of everything that was taking place. However, he quietly remained in his apartment, not making any sounds. Mona had done exactly what he had known she would do. She'd refused medical attention. She would do anything she could to protect his secret, even if it meant dying. In which case, she definitely would revive a vampire, which was want he wanted in the first place. Therefore, he was not all that concerned for her wellbeing.

He heard Harry clumping up the stairs with medicine for Mona's tummy. It was a kind gesture, but not one that would really help. Mona would simply have to ride it out, or succumb. It could go either way at this point. It mostly depended on her willpower and what she truly wanted.

Harry knocked on Mona's door and Michael let him inside. Gavril could hear the three humans doing what they could to make

Mona comfortable. They were goodhearted. That he liked about them. Then he heard Darren coming up the stairs. Gavril's eyes flashed red briefly. This one, he did not like. Although Darren, apparently, was sorry for the way he had ditched Mona, he was still very selfish and self-centered. Gavril harbored no delusions that if Mona were to go back to him, that Darren would, eventually, revert back to his true nature.

Matilda let Darren inside and he followed her to Mona's bedroom. He took one look. "My God! Dad, she needs medical attention!"

Michael was on the far side of the bed with Harry, who had just administered the medicine to Mona. "She doesn't want to go," Michael replied.

Mona weakly rolled her head towards Darren. "I will be all right. No doctors…" Her eyes closed then, and she was out.

"I have to agree," Matilda said, eyeing her husband as though he should do something. "Harry! You know more than the rest of us here. Do something!"

Darren noticed the bandage on Mona's neck. "What the hell is that?"

Michael replied, "Said she scraped her neck on a clothes hanger."

"Seriously?" Matilda asked. She reached over and took the large band aid by one of its edges and started to pull it back.

"What are you doing?" Harry asked.

"Maybe she has blood poisoning, Harry. Did you consider that?"

Apparently, the thought had not occurred to him. "Actually, no. I didn't know about the wound… until now."

Matilda zipped the bandage off then. They all froze temporarily. "Oh my God!" Matilda said, after finding her voice.

Two large holes, dark red with dried blood were on her neck.

"Looks like a snakebite," Darren remarked.

"One hell of a big snake," Michael noted.

Gavril poured himself a tall drink, smiling secretively to himself. Even if they were to figure out that it was a vampire bite, what could they do about it? He could kill them all in under two seconds. He figured that would not be necessary, not at that moment, anyway. Most humans did not believe vampires really did exist.

Then he heard Matilda say. "Vampire!"

"Hmmm… Seems I underestimated them," he said, grinning devilishly.

"You're not serious," Michael replied. "There are no such things as vampires, Matilda."

Harry spoke. "She watches every vampire flick, show, old or new, she can. Loves all that horror and supernatural stuff."

"There is some truth in all fiction!" she said defensively. "Get a doctor over here! Or take her to the hospital. See what they think."

"I have to agree with Matilda," Darren said. His eyes went to his father. "At least, on her being seen by a doctor."

Gavril sat his glass down. Time for him to act. He stood, straightened his collar and walked out of his apartment and knocked twice on Mona's door.

Michael answered the door. "Mr. Conta!"

"Count Conta… But please call me Gavril," he politely reminded.

"Sorry… Gavril."

"Is everything okay?" Gavril asked, sounding sincerely innocent. "I couldn't help but hear a number of people coming up and going into Mona's apartment. Kind of unusual. I thought Mona was working today. Is she all right?"

"Actually, she's not," Darren replied for his dad, as he appeared at his side. "She needs medical attention."

"Oh dear. What's wrong? Was she in an accident?"

Walking up, Matilda answered for the rest, "We don't know."

"Is there anything I can do?"

Michael and Darren shared a glance, and then Michael turned and answered, "Not really sure, Gavril. We were just debating on whether to take Mona to the hospital or call an ambulance."

"Would it be all right if I saw her?"

Michael glanced around at the others and back to Gavril. "I suppose so." He stepped sideways to allow Gavril entrance.

Feigning innocence, Gavril said, "I take it her bedroom's this way?" he indicated with an outstretched hand.

"Yes it is." Matilda replied, heading in first. Harry was still in the room.

"Oh my…" Gavril stated. "The poor thing is pale as a ghost." Pretending to just notice the two holes in her neck, he said, "Goodness! What happened here?" He held the hair away from her neck with the tips of his fingers and turned a very concerned frown to Michael.

"She said a clothes hanger," Michael replied.

Feigning incredulity, he said, "A clothes hanger?" He felt her forehead with his palm. "Cold as ice! No fever. That's good. However, her color is most disconcerting."

"You think?" Darren said, not trying very hard to hide his dislike of Gavril.

Gavril didn't care. "I agree. She should receive medical attention." This was not something he would have desired, but too many humans were in on his business now. He had two choices: kill them all or make the situation work in his favor. And since Mona cared about these humans, he opted for the latter.

"She's going to be really upset with us," Michael said, "but I agree, too."

"Let's not waste another second," Gavril said, pulling a yellow iPhone out of his hip pocket. He called 911 and requested an ambulance.

A few minutes later, the ambulance arrived and the still unconscious Mona was carted off on a gurney. Michael and Darren rode in the ambulance with Mona. Harry and Matilda retuned to the store to take care of several disgruntled customers. Gavril said that he would see Mona at the hospital later.

Chapter Seven:

If Darren disliked Count Conta before, he really detested him now – the smugness, the superior air he exuded. He sensed that besides having his dad for competition, this weird stranger was somehow a threat, not only in possibly taking Mona away from them, but there was that other thing about him: Whatever it was that gave one the Heebie Jeebies. In fact, the man scared the hell out of him.

In Mona's hospital room, Darren sat in a corner chair close to the door, toes down, nervously bouncing his heels up and down.

Michael had gone out for coffee, but when he returned, he sat Darren a cup down on a small table. He couldn't help but notice Darren's feet still bouncing. "Could you please stop that?"

Darren looked up. "Huh?"

"Your feet, Darren. You're driving me nuts."

"Oh!" he slipped his feet out in front of the chair and leaned back. "Sorry. Antsy, worried about Mona."

Michael eased down on the side of Mona's bed. She was still out. He sipped on his coffee and sat his Styrofoam cup down on the stand by the bed. "You're still focusing on the Count, aren't you?"

"Yeah… I am. As much as I hate to admit it, he did show concern for Mona this evening. Did what any of us would have done. However, you're right. I don't trust the man. Gives me the creeps."

"He *is* a foreigner, Darren."

"It's more than that."

"I can practically see the wheels turning in your head… Out with it son."

He went to speak, but a tall blond doctor with gray eyes and sculptured features walked in. Doctor Jamison was on his name tag.

"Evening gentlemen," he said, moving over to Mona's bed and picking up her wrist to feel her pulse. "Hmmm." He gently laid her arm back on the bed and released it. Then he viewed her chart. "Strange," he said, as though to himself, not to the two men in the room.

"You have any ideas what's wrong with her doctor?" Michael inquired.

His snorting laugh had a cynical tone. "Actually, I know one thing that's wrong with her, but for the life of me, I cannot figure out the cause."

"What is that, doctor?" Darren asked, standing now.

"She's lost a lot of blood. A whole lot!" He no sooner said it and a couple of nurses came in. One held a unit of blood; the other had a couple of syringes filled with medicine.

Darren shot a concerned glance to his dad.

The doctor spoke. "You two wouldn't know how she acquired these strange holes in her neck, would you?"

"She said," Michael answered, "that it was from a clothes hanger. One of those old fashioned wire clothes hangers."

Doctor Jamison eyed him curiously. "I take it by your tone that you don't quite buy that explanation as to how it really happened?"

"Honestly, no. I sure as hell don't."

"Well, there aren't any other wounds on her body. She had to have bled out through these two holes, which is quite likely. Especially, since it was directly in the carotid artery. Funny thing is, her heart should have pumped her dry and it didn't! Something stopped the bleeding. I have to say she's one lucky young lady. By rights, she should be dead now. But she is alive. Weak, I admit, but alive."

"Oh my God!" Michael exclaimed. "I had no idea it was *that* close of a call for her."

The doctor laid his clipboard aside. "Honestly," he said, smiling ambiguously, "if I didn't know better, I would say she was attacked by a vampire."

Darren had taken a sip of his coffee. Hearing the doctor's words, he choked, spewing his coffee everywhere. He quickly apologized and grabbed some tissues out of a box on the side table.

Michael spoke, "You're kidding, right? You don't *seriously* believe it was a vampire, do you, Doctor Jamison?"

"I have to say this, I don't believe in them. Never have. I've always been a practical, down to earth, individual. Still, I have never seen wounds like these. Not in the twenty years I have been practicing my craft."

"Is it feasible that the holes could have been inflicted by a clothes hanger?"

He thought about it a moment. "No. Not even just one hole. A clothes hanger would have probably caused more of a tear at some point. The holes are too clean. And for there to be two perfectly aligned holes, damn near impossible. I would be more willing to believe they were inflicted by a giant snake. However, I don't think that is what happened. For one, a giant snake would more than likely be a constrictor... Would squeeze its victim. There are no bruises or cracked bones. Nope. Not a snake."

Darren spoke, "Then what on earth could have done it?"

The doctor picked up the clipboard and faced the two men. "Right now, your guess is as good as mine. Tell me, does she have any relatives around?"

"Her mother lives in Bremerton," Darren replied. I phoned her while ago. She should be on her way here."

"Good. Best to have some family around... just in case complications arise."

"Complications?" Michael asked.

"I don't foresee any. We have her on antibiotics and we gave her a tetanus shot," he said, nodding towards the middle-aged female nurse that had just administered the shots and was tossing the needles in the metal 'sharps' container. "Still, there is the big question of how it happened. That one, if you figure out before I do, please let me know."

"Certainly, doctor."

Just then, there was a timid knock on the door. "Come on in," Doctor Jamison said.

Gloria Sims rushed in all flustered and worried, pulling a red silk scarf off her head and nodding to everyone, and went straight over to her daughter. "Dear God! She's so pale."

"Believe it or not," the doctor said. "Her color is beginning to get better. We just got the transfusion going a few minutes ago."

She spun around, removing her brown coat and handing it and the scarf over to Michael to hang in the closet for her. "I don't understand?"

It was then that Michael said he and Darren would get going, now that she was there.

"All right." She hugged both men and thanked Darren for calling.

"Of course, Mrs. Sims."

They walked out of the room, and the doctor went to explaining to Gloria all that he knew of her daughter's condition.

Gavril waited in the lobby, hiding behind a newspaper, until Michael and his father left, he wanted to see Mona alone, but he knew the minute he stepped off the elevator on her floor that she was not alone. There was someone with her, a woman. He surmised that it might be her mother or another relative. He decided to go on in, but he stayed only a minute, quickly introducing himself as Mona's neighbor, and saying he just wanted to pay her a short visit to see how she was. Gloria thanked him for dropping by, and he returned home.

Gloria Sims would probably hang around for a day or two; at least until she was convinced Mona was okay. It was a minor setback for Gavril, but he wasn't too upset. After all, he had all the time in the world.

The following morning, after three units of blood and looking a lot healthier, Doctor Jamison let Mona go home, with the promise from her mother that she would look after her for a few days.

Gavril wasn't real pleased with having the woman over there, but he wasn't unhappy either. He was glad Mona had a mother who genuinely cared for her. In his seemingly countless years, he had seen plenty who didn't. He made his own efforts to be the good neighbor, checking in on them from time to time, and Matilda made sure they had plenty of soup and homemade bread to eat. Harry checked on her a couple of times a day.

After three days, Mona was feeling as fit as ever and said she was ready to return to work. So, with a warm hug and a goodbye, Gloria left her daughter early the next Monday morning.

Gavril was out in the hall (intentionally), newspaper tucked under his arm and coffee in hand. He bid her a good morning, and with a cheerful reply she left to catch her ferry. He was anxious to see Mona alone, but he could hear her rushing around readying for work. He would wait a little while longer. There was no real hurry. Anyway, they would have to begin the transitioning all over again. Only it wouldn't take as long this time. Even though she had been given new blood, some of his still flowed in her veins. She was still linked to him, under his willpower, and would be for some time to come. Even if she wanted to, she would tell no one of his being a vampire, for that was inherent; a protective mechanism passed on to his victims. She would still be drawn to him, though, whether she was in love with him or not.

Ready for work, Mona hurried out her door but stopped cold and stared at Gavril's door, remembering all that she could of the past few days – He was a vampire! *A vampire!* Because of him, she had almost died. Because of him, her whole life was turned upside down. Because of him, she was lying to her friends and her mother. Logic, reasoning, told her to get away from him while she could, to run, run, and run some more. It was all so crazy! So unbelievable! Still, the most insane part of it all was the fact that she *wanted* to be with him. Every bone and sinew in her body wanted him to take her in his powerful arms and make wild, unbridled love to her, and while he did, to drink from her. As she stood there, she realized she ached. Ached terribly. She ached for him! "Gavril…" she whispered, knowing full well he could hear.

He materialized in front of her, smiling down at her in his charming, electric way. "My sweet." He gently wrapped his arms around her and kissed her lovingly.

She gasped as he pulled away; her eyes glued to his. "I don't want to leave you," she admitted.

His eyes crinkled, smiling. "Today, you must. Everyone has put forth too much effort to… to help you. They do not understand, nor will they ever." He stroked her hair on the side of her head. "You should go to work today. Let everyone see you looking so well."

She bobbed her head, knowing full well he spoke the truth. "Okay. But I don't want to."

"That's my girl."

"Will I see you tonight?"

"Nothing on the earth will keep you from it, my sweet. Go to work. Do what you must. Focus on your job. And tonight… tonight I promise to take you to the very stars."

Her face brightened. "…All right."

He checked his Rolex. "I suggest you get going. Or you'll be running late." He dissipated into thin air.

"Jeeze! I wish I could do that."

"You will be able too soon, my sweet," she heard him say.

"Okay," she breathed and headed down the stairs.

Darren ran into Starbucks to grab a mocha. Right away he noticed the cute little strawberry blonde with brown eyes standing in line just in front of him. He'd seen her there before. She was a high school student, went to the school that was just a couple of blocks over. She turned and recognized his as a familiar face and offered him a sweet smile, which he instantly reflected.

"I'm running a little late this morning," she said in her pleasant voice.

"Makes two of us," he replied. "My alarm didn't go off this morning. Think I must have turned over, shut it off and went back to sleep."

"I've done that before."

The barista had the girl's coffee ready. She paid for it, smiled and wished Darren a good day.

"You too," he said, eyeing her tight derriere in skinny jeans, as she hurried out the door on her way to school. Right away, his thoughts went where they shouldn't. *No! Can't do that again. Can't!*

"Your mocha, sir," the little Hispanic barista said, getting his attention.

He turned back around. "Thanks!" He grabbed his coffee and went on out the door. He just couldn't help it; he looked down the walk to his left. The girl was rounding the corner. "No, Darren," he said under his breath. "You must not do it again!" He shifted his focus on work, which was only a couple of doors down. He, most definitely, could not afford to do that again. He'd already gotten away with it twice. He figured a third time would be his lucky – unlucky – charm. "Three… and you're out!" he said under his breath.

Michael was hanging up his coat when Mona breezed in, looking a hundred percent better than she had only a couple of days ago. "Morning, Mona," he said, eyes smiling. "You have no idea how good you look right now."

She stopped midway to her office door to reply. "Thank you, Michael." She sucked in air and exhaled. "You know, I want to thank you and Darren for being there for me when I needed someone."

"Mona…" His eyes misted over. "We almost lost you! I don't ever want to go through anything like that again."

She shrugged apologetically. "I'm sorry. I didn't mean to scare everyone… Really."

He moved up to her, gently resting his hands on her shoulders. "My God! Don't apologize. It wasn't your fault." There was a marginal shift in his expression. "Do you remember at all what happened to you? How you got those two… rather large holes in your neck?"

His question seemed to make her nervous. She glanced off. "I told you. Got it caught on a coat hanger."

He gently pulled her face back around with his fingertips. "You almost bled to death, Mona. Why didn't you seek help?"

"I did," she replied, voice edging on the defensive. "I got medicine from Harry."

It was more than obvious that she was lying, but for whatever reason, she wasn't going to tell the truth. His probing questions were only upsetting her. "Okay. It's okay. I won't ask you again. Just know this: If there is anything you decide you want to tell me… or not, I am here for you."

Overhearing his dad, while walking by, Darren popped his head in. "We're both here for you, Mona."

Nodding appreciatively but still uncomfortable, she replied, "Thank you! I'm lucky to have you two watching over me. Not to mention Harry and Matilda. I'm okay now. You needn't worry about me anymore. In fact, I am anxious to return to work."

"Great!" Darren said. "I need to get over to the courthouse… like fifteen minutes ago." He disappeared.

Michael took a step back, checking his watch. "We have an hour and then we need to be there, as well."

"All right." She went on to her office.

Michael couldn't help but notice that Mona failed to mention Gavril Conta, for he had been there for her too. Was it a coincidence that she forgot to mention him? Or did she deliberately leave him out of the conversation, for some reason or the other? He had the strangest feeling that Gavril knew a whole lot more about what was going on than what was being said. He was beginning to think that Darren's suspicions about the man had some validity.

Just as Michael was putting on his coat to leave for the courthouse, Mona stepped into his office, ready to go. "I was at my mother's."

"What?" he replied, not knowing what she was talking about.

"The sixteenth of August. You asked me if I could remember what Darren and I were doing that day."

"Oh yeah! I did." He pulled his coat together in front, hands clasping his lapels. "You were at your mother's?" His countenance darkened marginally.

"Yes! I didn't remember offhand, but I looked back at my calendar in the kitchen. I had marked it off. Darren was supposed to go with me, but said he had some things he needed to attend to."

"Were you there the whole day?"

"Until ten p.m. Then I had to catch the late ferry. I remember now. I almost missed it."

"That was the Friday you took the whole day off. Right?"

"Yes. Why?"

"I thought so, but I wasn't sure. I knew Darren took it off too. But you say he didn't go with you?"

"No," she replied, eyeing him strangely. "He didn't. I was a little miffed at him too. He had promised."

"I see," he said, jaw twitching. He blew out air. "Well, Judge Whitaker isn't going to wait. We'd best get going." He held out a hand for her to lead the way.

Mona watched Michael in court. His usual self-confidence was still in tack, and he was just as swift as ever, but she knew he was beginning to suspect what she suspected – that Darren was the man who had raped the Gilbert and Landsbury girls. What other reason could he have wanted to know what she and Darren were doing August sixteenth? When he had first asked about it, it had not clicked, but when she thought about it, she realized that was the day the Gilbert girl had been raped. Apparently, Michael had gone over the Tim Brown file thoroughly. In which case, there was no way he could have missed the mention of the birthmark on Brown's chest – the birthmark that didn't exist, at least on Tim Brown, or on Rick Harrison.

As she observed him, she couldn't help but feel sympathetic. He was such a good man and great lawyer. She knew there was another son, older. She thought his name was Richard, but Michael rarely mentioned him. He was a doctor, a neurologist. Married to another doctor, a gynecologist, and they had a young, three-year-old son, Timothy, the only grandchild in the family. Michael and Richard weren't that close, though. Not as close as Michael and Darren were, even with Darren being so spoiled. From what she could ascertain, from what Darren had flippantly mentioned a time or two in conversation, was that Richard always thought Darren got away with too much. It was one of the reasons he had chosen to move to the other side of the country.

Michael deserved better. That she did not doubt. What's more, she felt that if the mysterious Gavril had not come into her life, she would, more than likely, be with Michael right now, even though he was old enough to be her father. Until recently, she would have never even entertained the idea of being in a romantic relationship with someone so much older. She had to admit, though, that he was very attractive and certainly did not look to be almost fifty-one. Had she not known his age, she would have guessed him to be between forty and forty-five.

He realized she had been watching him intently, for when he went to take a seat and the prosecuting attorney came up, he looked at her straight on and smiled warmly. She knew then that he had mistaken her staring as something more. She had not meant to encourage him. Now that she was with Gavril, being with Michael in the way he wanted was out of the question.

A low layer of dark clouds draped over the city and it was raining heavily. According to the weather station, the rain would continue the rest of the afternoon and on into late evening, possibly through the night. Gavril, pleased with the forecast, stood from his easy chair and took his glass to the kitchen sink. There was little doubt but what he could safely go out into the world. It was days like this that he cherished, and one of the reasons he had chosen Seattle to live for a while – the rain and cloudy weather it was so notorious for. Having to live his life primarily at night was the only thing that really 'sucked' about being a vampire. He chuckled softly, musing the pun over in his head.

Tired of vodka and gin, he wanted something different, until he could satisfy his thirst for blood. He skipped down the stairwell and into the drugstore, where he was cheerily greeted by Harry and Matilda, even though they were busy with customers. He waved warmly and moved on to the glass front door, peered out momentarily, and then walked out into what was as much daylight he could ever tolerate without instantly blistering from head to toe. The rain was coming down heavily, so he shrugged his head down inside the collar of his water-repellent trench coat and headed for Starbucks. A hot mocha sounded very inviting right now.

The clock hanging on the wall over the barista's shoulder had its short hand on the twelve and the long hand on the two, a little past noon. The door swung wide and a cute little strawberry blonde, hair halfway down to her buttocks, apparently a high school student, burst in and stepped in line behind him.

Gavril was next, so he ordered his mocha. Just then, a familiar figure breezed in the front door, but as soon as Gavril was noticed, he stopped cold in his tracks. Gavril smiled smugly at Darren, took his coffee that was ready, and walked on over to an empty table and sat down to enjoy his hot beverage and observe the coffee lovers in there for their caffeine fix for the afternoon.

The strawberry blonde paid for her coffee and moved to a table by the door. Darren was in the process of ordering his, but he kept glancing at the girl – who was not looking at him – and then he took a chance glance at Gavril – who was, and he quickly turned his attention back to the barista. Soon as he had his coffee, he looked towards the girl again, but she still seemed to either not see him, or she was ignoring him. Gavril sensed it was the latter. After all, Darren was just a bit old for the young lady, who didn't look a day over fifteen.

"Interesting," Gavril said under his breath where no one could hear. "Interesting, indeed." He drained his coffee cup and sat it down, deciding to linger, to stick around and see what Darren would do.

Darren stood there for a few moments, not looking real sure of what to do. It was plain to Gavril that the man wanted to approach the girl, but she wasn't encouraging him, and Gavril's presence was definitely making him nervous. Darren finally turned and looked at Gavril straight on. It was apparent that he had made his mind up not to let Gavril's being there stop him. He stepped on up to the girl, who looked up at last.

"Oh! Hi!" she said.

"May I?" he asked, gesturing with his coffee hand towards the chair across from hers.

She didn't look too sure, but didn't want to be rude, so said, "Sure."

He broke into a satisfied smile, glancing only briefly at Gavril before focusing back on the girl.

"I take it you come here for your lunch break? I'm not in here a lot, but I've seen you in here before at this time."

She nodded yes, sipping on her coffee before setting it down. "Yes. Not every day, but I come in almost daily."

"What I thought."

She glanced at her watch. "Well, I have ten minutes to walk back to school. I'd better run."

"Oh? Ok!" he responded in surprise. The girl was nervous. "Well, have a good rest of the day!"

"I will. Thank you!" She smiled sweetly, glanced at Gavril, whom she apparently had noticed watching them, and then dashed on out the door.

Darren sat there for a few seconds, looking a bit embarrassed and flustered. After a moment, he muttered, "To hell with it!" and wasted not a second in rushing out the door.

Gavril watched with keen interest. Darren went off to his right, in the opposite direction of the girl. Instinct told Gavril, that had he not been there, Darren would have followed her. He decided right then and there that if the girl came up harmed or missing that Darren was a dead man. Though a killer himself, harming children was an anathema to him.

He stood, tossed his cup in a trash bin and walked out into the pelting rain. He went to the left, making himself invisible and followed the girl to the campus. Once she was inside the building, safe, he went on his way. He wanted to browse around Pike Place Market and enjoy the sights and scents – the flower and herb shops, curios, trinkets and whatnots – in the daylight, a rare privilege for him. One that humans took for granted.

Michael and Mona made it back to the office shortly before five. The day had been full of court cases, and they'd barely had time to grab lunch. Michael tidied up his desk and Mona slipped inside her office to do the same. When she came out, he was waiting for her.

Seeing he wanted to say something, she stopped. "Yes? What is it, Michael?"

"Could we try it again?"

She closed her eyes briefly before opening them again and responding. "I like you a lot, Michael. But I really don't think so."

"Mona… I'm so sorry."

She put up a hand. "Don't! Please! I care for you. I think I always will."

"Then what is the harm in giving me… us… another chance?"

She faced him squarely. "I told you. There is someone else." She bit her lip, studying him as though she wanted to say more, but didn't. "I'm sorry. I have to go now." She turned away.

"Gavril?" he asked.

"Yes!" she replied without looking back at him. "You knew that already."

"You're right. I did. But I had to ask."

She wriggled her head and walked out.

He gave her a few minutes to go ahead, not wanting to make her uncomfortable. With a heavy heart, he would ride the next elevator down. He had come so close! So close! But he'd let her slip right through his hands. When he exited the building, he just stood there under the canopy watching the driving rain. The weather suited his dark mood. He thought about it a minute. At least, she wasn't dead. That would have been the only thing worse than what he was feeling right now. He thanked God that she was still alive and, apparently, okay. With that thought, he pulled his black collapsible umbrella out of his inside coat pocket, opened it, and dashed off to get his car out of the parking garage.

Mona expected Gavril to be home when she got there; expected him to come knocking on her door at any minute, but to her surprise, an hour passed with no word from him. Surely he had heard her come in. After all, didn't he have acute hearing? He was a vampire. Did he not know she was home?

After a while, Mona gave up expecting him and made herself half a tuna sandwich, as she'd mostly lost her appetite now, disappointed that he hadn't been waiting for her to come home. Only, where was he? She sat down in front of her television with her half sandwich and a glass of tea. She would attempt to lose herself in the evening news.

When he left the office for the day, Darren stopped off at the Starbucks again, hoping the pretty strawberry blonde had come there after school. She wasn't there when he arrived, but he took out his laptop and decided to scan over some of his notes and drink his coffee, hoping she would show up. He sat there for a half hour with her as a no-show. "Oh hell with it!" He put his laptop in its case and stood, taking his empty cup and disposing it in the trash can by the door. That was when he realized that Gavril was sitting at a small table on the other side of the door. Darren stopped in his tracks. Those obsidian eyes seemed to be mocking him, holding him locked in their cold stare. He had a sudden hard chill. Barely conscious of swallowing the lump that had formed in his throat; he swiftly turned and ran out the door. "Oh jeeze!" he uttered; now running to the garage to get his car.

When he reached the third level of the garage, he saw something he'd never seen there before: A thick, low-lying fog all over the concrete floor where his car was parked. "Huh?" he scratched the back of his head in bewilderment. He had noticed fog on the ground earlier, but thought it had disappeared. But fog up here? He made a hundred-and-eighty-degree turn. "What the hell?" The fog seemed to be rising. A terrible foreboding enveloped him. He ran over to his car and couldn't back out of there fast enough, almost hitting a little red Honda pulling out of the second level. In a panic, he laid on his horn, but the brunette driving the car gave him the finger and sped off. "Bitch!" he screamed and suddenly realized he was hysterical. Daring a quick glance out his side window, he noticed the fog seemed to be following him. "What the fuck is going on?" At last, he reached the opening and drove out into the street.

No fog!

He slammed on his brakes and pulled over to an opening at the curb. There he sat for several minutes, waiting for his racing heart to slow down and for his breathing to ease. He realized he was white-knuckling the steering wheel. "Got to get a hold of myself. Got too! I am losing it. Must be! None of this is really happening. I'm just losing it. Got to get a hold of myself. *Got too!"* he practically screamed.

Recognizing that he was in no shape to drive just yet, he pulled out his cell phone and called Nancy. Just hearing her voice, hearing her gripe at him in her normal, criticizing way, was at least something he could deal with. He sat there letting her complain about his lack of consideration for not calling her and telling her he was going to be late. "Yeah… Yeah…" he replied, just focusing on the normal, not wanting to consider the abnormal. "Sorry. I'll be home as soon as possible. Stuck in traffic." That appeased her and they said their goodbyes. He returned his phone back to his pocket and sat there for a few more minutes watching cars drive by and people out on the sidewalks going in and out of the buildings across the street. The fog seemed to be gone. That, in itself, made him feel better. He studied his still trembling hands. Not quite a bad as they were only a few minutes ago. Perhaps now, he could drive home without wrecking the car. He started it up again, looked for an opening in the traffic and headed for home.

Having had his fun, Gavril returned home. As soon as he walked in the front door of the drugstore, he picked up Mona's disappointment that he had not been there. Pleased, a devilish smile formed on his lips.

Matilda saw him from behind the perfume counter and bid him a cheerful good evening.

"Evening," he replied. Harry was too engrossed with filling prescriptions to notice or hear. Gavril went on to the back and up the stairs. He quietly slipped into his apartment, not wanting Mona to know he was home just yet. He wanted to change into dry clothes, as it was still raining pretty heavily yet, and have a drink before seeing her.

Nancy stood at the refrigerator trying to decide what they might have for supper when Darren came in. He tossed his briefcase and laptop on the sofa and headed straight over to the kitchen, took her in his arms and planted her with a big kiss. She was thoroughly surprised and it showed in her face when he pulled back.

"What gives?" she asked.

"Just want you to know how much I appreciate you."

"…Why thank you!" Brow furrowed, she reached up and gently stroked his wet bangs away from his forehead. "You've never said anything like that to me before… Are you okay?"

"Now that I am with you, I am."

"Want to tell me about it?"

"I just kind of panicked when I got off work. I don't know… Maybe I've been so uptight that my father might find out about those tampered files that I'm imagining things."

"Imagining what things?" She said, turning back to the refrigerator.

"Fog in the parking garage."

She turned her head sideways, studying his taut face.

"Fog on the third floor!"

At once frowning slightly with concern, she said, "That is kind of weird. But I suppose you can have fog anywhere. Isn't fog just a low cloud?"

"Yes. It's just … I'm just crazy."

She forgot about the refrigerator and hung her arms around his neck. "You're not crazy. You need to stop worrying about that file, Darren. I am sure everything is going to be okay."

With a shift of his eyebrows, he said, "I hope you're right."

She turned to the refrigerator once more.

"Forget about cooking. Let's go to Outback."

"Sounds good to me. I really didn't want to cook anyway."

"I know you hate to cook, even though you are a good one."

"Seriously? You think so?"

"Seriously. I think you make the best pot roast I've ever eaten."

She smiled then like he'd never seen her smile before. "Gee! I thought you didn't like my cooking. After all, I've never, seriously, considered myself the domestic type."

"Actually, I love your cooking. I just know you don't like to cook. So, I don't encourage it."

She laughed. "Well, it makes me feel good to know that. I really wouldn't mind cooking more, if I thought you really did love my cooking."

"Not kidding. You are an awesome cook!"

"That settles it. I have a couple T-bones in the freezer that I can thaw in the microwave, and I'll make a tossed salad."

"Sounds awesome."

"Baked potato okay?"

"With steak, hell yeah."

She kissed him quickly and went to preparing their dinner. He went off to change into dry clothes.

Margaret finished off her martini and set the glass down on the bar, turned and stared at her husband, who'd been sitting in the living room for the past hour, looking very subdued and lost in thought. The television was on, but he wasn't paying any attention to it. She blew out air. "Michael! For God's sake! What's wrong?"

He snapped his head up. "What?"

"You're still pining over Mona, aren't you?"

"Am I?" He shook his head in exasperation. "I don't know if it's that or if I'm just worried about this guy... this new neighbor of hers."

"You sure you're not just jealous, Michael?"

She moved over to join him on the sofa. "You can talk to me, you know?"

He eyed her quizzically. "I know the little talk we had before. You still think we might have a chance?"

"I have really been thinking my life over these last few days, Michael. Richard is on the other side of the country with his wife and kid. We never see them. I'd like to see my grandson and our oldest son once in a while. I know I've been in denial for some time, but I know why he moved away."

Michael turned his head toward hers. "Why, Margaret?"

"You know how he feels about our spoiling Darren. It's not just that. He detests the whole social circle thing we... I've... been addicted to for years."

"I know. He's never minced words about it."

"To change the subject. Are you really worried about Mona?"

"Couldn't be more worried."

"What is it about this guy, anyway?"

"I'm not really sure. He's just strange. I know Darren is a little scared of him."

"We both know Darren's always been a bit of a worm... but that's probably our fault."

"Not sure that's it. I've met this guy. There is something a little spooky about him. I can't say what it is, though."

She thought about it a minute. "You don't really put any meat into what the doctor commented, do you? About a vampire being responsible for those holes in her neck? He was just being... facetious, wasn't he?"

"That's what common sense tells me, Margaret. Still, there is something not right about him. I feel it in my bones."

She leaned forward and grabbed her cigarettes off the coffee table, took one out and lit it with the black Bic that was on the table. She blew out smoke to the side and leaned back. "Being a lawyer all these years, Michael, has given you an acute sense about people. If you say there is something not right about this guy, then I believe you."

"Thank you for that much, Margaret."

She took another drag from her cigarette, again blowing the smoke off to the side, so as not to get in his face. "You really are in love with her, aren't you?"

He studied her dark brown eyes, her stare was steady. She wasn't being flippant or hateful. She was sincere. "Yes! I'm in love with her. I know I'm too old for her, though. I have no business wanting to be with a woman in her early twenties."

"Hey! The movie stars don't seem to have a problem with it."

He couldn't help himself, it was the way she said it, made him chuckle. "You do have a point." He sighed. "You know, I almost get the feeling you care."

"I told you the other day, how I felt. I do care about you. You're my husband. Whether we stay together or not, I will always have a special place for you in my heart.'

He went to speak, but she shushed him.

"Let me finish. I'll admit I'm not in love with you anymore. However, I do love you. We've been through too much. We've put one another through too much. Especially, me giving you hell, but as rotten as I've sometimes been, I *do* care, and I always have."

Her comment was so unexpected, it totally took him by surprise and tears came to his eyes. "Margaret…"

"I didn't mean to make you cry."

He reached over and took the cigarette from her fingers and put it out it in the ashtray on the coffee table. "Come here."

She cocked her head questioningly. "What?"

"This." He took her in his arms and kissed her sweetly.

She let out a little groan and reciprocated, returning his kiss. He pulled back then, taking her hand and stood. She stood too. With a nod towards the bedroom, he asked, "Shall we?"

Her eyes misted over too. She smiled softly. "Yes."

Arm in arm, they slowly made their way to their bedroom.

Chapter Eight:

Mona glanced at the time on her phone. *Ten p.m.!* Suddenly, she was pissed. Just the night before, Gavril had promised, in his words, 'To take you to the very stars". It had been all she could do to make it through the day until she could go home to him, believing he would be there anxiously anticipating her arrival.

Only he had not been here. She had not heard from him all evening. Wasn't tonight to be their night? She seriously doubted that anything had happened to him. After all, he was a five-hundred-year-old vampire! He'd survived all these years. She seriously doubted that anything was wrong with him. She went to take her shower, slamming her bedroom door as she went.

Across the hall, a deep chuckle arose in Gavril's chest. She was ready.

Earlier, he had slipped into a blood bank and helped himself to a couple of units of blood to give to her when the time came. He thirsted, but planned on drinking his fill from her. Tonight, he would make passionate love to her and then drain her to the point of death, but leave her just enough blood, now mixed with his. She would die, of course, but his blood was in her, regardless, and she would come back a vampire – A very thirsty vampire. If he didn't have something to offer her right away, she could go on a killing spree that might be difficult to hide. This, he did not want to happen. Maintaining anonymity was of utmost importance, for most of the world believed vampires to be a myth. If the truth were to get out, folks would panic, and probably kill innocent people. The thought brought memories of the Salem witch trials to mind. Sometimes the ignorance of the masses went way beyond reason. What's more, it would be harder to hide and keep ones true nature a secret. Couldn't let that happen. At the most, Mona could possibly have a few rough days, but it would soon pass, and then they would be free to move on. However, with his coaxing and guidance, she should make the transition without too much of a problem and, hopefully, they could move on quickly.

He had already sent Maxmillian an email from the local library to let him know he would soon be bringing home a new mate. At which Maxmillian had responded with a most enthusiastic letter, pleased his master was happy once more.

It was Gavril's wish to take Mona back to Romania to visit the old castle first, where his cousin Dracula once lived; wanted to show her the sights and tell her of all the things that he had lived through in his many years. Yes. Tired of the loneliness and seclusion, he looked forward to having a mate once more. He hoped that this one would be with him until the end of their time, however long or short that might be; for he had known of a few who had lived, not only to a thousand, but several thousand years. Hell. He had been just a youngster to them.

He would let her stew a little while longer though. There was something he wanted to do first. The human Darren was a danger to innocent young girls. The vibes he had picked up from the man when he was checking out the girl at Starbucks were not good. Even though he, himself, was evil by his very vampire nature, he would never harm a child. That went against his principles.

He planned on paying the younger Graves a little visit before he focused on Mona; shake him up a little bit. He wanted his mind clear and free from everything else when he made love to her.

Nancy finished loading the dishwasher and thought she heard a dog howling in the distance. She paid little heed to it at first, but then another dog joined in. The next thing she knew, a whole chorus of dogs were howling, including ones in their neighborhood. She glanced out the window. Though the sky had cleared and the moon was full and bright, she noticed a heavy fog rolling in low to the ground. "Weird." Fog was not something unusual in Seattle, but to have a clear sky above and heavy fog on the ground was not so common. "Darren," she called, for he was in the study preparing a case for the next day.

He didn't answer at first. She stood there watching the fog churn as it seemed to be spreading out all around their yard. It was eerie, had a bluish cast, making it appear other worldly. "Darren!" she said again.

This time he answered. "What?"

"Can't you hear them?"

"Yeah!" he suddenly replied. "What the hell is going on?" His footfalls could be heard as he came down the hall to the kitchen.

"I don't know," she replied, still standing in front of the window. "Maybe that fog's creeping them out?"

Just glancing out from behind her, he didn't see it at first. "But the sky's clear?"

"Not the sky. The ground!" She gestured for him to step up and look towards the ground.

"Crap! That is a little spooky."

"You're telling me," she said, turning to him. "Reminds me of the fog in one of those classic Lon Chaney, werewolf flicks."

The howling had grown to almost a deafening pitch. Lights that had been out were now on all over the neighborhood.

Nancy covered her ears. "My God! Not sure I can take much more of this!"

"Me either!" He stepped back from the window.

Then suddenly it stopped and everything grew strangely quiet. They shared an uneasy glance. "Darren, I'm a little freaked out here."

It was apparent that he was as uneasy as she, but he wanted to be the protective male. He inserted an arm around her waist. "Come on. The howling's stopped. Let's just go to bed and hope it doesn't start up again."

With an agreeing nod, she let him escort her back to their bedroom.

With the lights out, neither saw the dark fingers of smoke working and wriggling their way under and around the window seals. Soon it was completely inside and formed into the shadow of a man in a far dark corner – Gavril. He watched with interest while the couple made love, and when they were done, they turned over and soon fell asleep. A wicked smile traced his lips. He waited until they were both in deep sleep, and then he moved up to

Darren, placing a hand ever so gently on his forehead, sending him into a much deeper sleep; one that he would not easily awaken from, until Gavril was ready to wake him.

In a breath, Gavril was beside Nancy. She was a physically lovely woman, but he knew her type: selfish and immature, not really caring for the wellbeing of others, unless they were close to her. Without her even being aware of him, he slipped into the bed beside her. He lay there for a minute, smiling wickedly to himself, and then gently slipping her gown up out of the way (she hadn't bothered to put on her panties) he took her before she knew what was happening –thought that it was Darren taking seconds – screwing her in a most passionate way, like nothing she had ever experienced before.

She had no clue that she was being ravaged by a vampire; wasn't sure if Darren was making love to her or if she was having a wonderful, erotic dream. Spreading her legs willfully and arching up to his every move, she moaned in ecstasy, as he delighted and had his way with her. Then, just as she came around, he sunk his fangs deep into the soft flesh of her neck and drank from her while she vibrated, enraptured beneath him. She moaned here and there, but her desire far exceeded her pain, still unaware she was being ravaged by a monster. Drinking all he wanted from her, as he wanted to partake of Mona when he returned home, he released his pleasure into her. She lay there writhing in the euphoria of his touch.

He waited until they were both completely finished, before ripping open his wrist and feeding her just enough of his blood to give her some strength, as his intent was not to kill her, and then he was instantly off of her and standing by her side of the bed. Her neck was bleeding profusely. It would stop soon, though, as his saliva would cause the wound to close. Weakened, she had fallen unconscious, as well. He stood there, smiling naughtily down at his victim, and then he laid a hand on Darren's head again, bringing him out of his deep slumber. Satisfied that he'd left his calling card, he dissipated. It was time to go home to Mona.

Pissed, discouraged, outraged and totally beside herself, Mona threw her covers back and stomped off to the bathroom to pee. She couldn't sleep. All she could do was think about Gavril and wonder why in hell he had done this to her. It was one thing to be dumped by Darren, but to be dumped by a freakin', awesome vampire was totally another! "I'll never get over this! Never! Talk about adding insult to injury! This is the epitome of insults! If I could kill him, I would. Only, I think he's already dead. Or undead? Shit! I don't know." She relieved herself and looked in her bathroom mirror. She was pretty. Maybe not the tall, classy kind of bitch Nancy was. Still, though average in height, five-foot-five, she was pretty. "What is wrong with me?" she said to the mirror. "What is it about me that men want to fuck me and then dump me? Ugh!" She stomped back to her bed and was just about to get back in under the covers when she realized someone was standing at the foot of her bed. She just about jumped out of her skin.

"Jeeze!" She yelled. Then she saw it was Gavril. He was smiling as though he found her anger amusing. "What are you smiling about? And why did you stand me up tonight?"

He suppressed a laugh before calmly replying, "I did not stand you up, my love. I just had something to take care of first."

"You could have let me know, you know."

His black eyes of marble held her gaze fixedly. "You must learn to trust me, Mona. As my mate, I will never betray you. At least, as long as you stand by my side and take heed to and learn all that I need to teach you. You must listen and obey until such a time that you are thoroughly schooled in what it truly means to be a creature of the night, such as I, a vampire. Then, *only* then, will I be able to let you go unfettered about the world.

"I'm listening. Still, I'm a little hurt. You could have let me know."

His eyes twinkled and his complacent grin grew. "Just know this. You do not have to worry about me 'dumping' you." An eyebrow arched. "Not my style. Not going to happen. That is, unless you deliberately betray me. Then you won't live long enough to worry about it."

"Oh!" she gulped. His mood tonight was different than she'd witnessed of him before. Found him a little scary. Still, she wanted him, wanted him to the point of madness.

He knew this and instantly was in her face, delving black eyes into her very soul. "I will drink my last drink of you as a human tonight."

Another gulp, but she nodded that she was ready.

"There is no backing out now, Mona. Understood?"

Her eyes were wide with fright, but she trembled for his mere touch. Every nerve in her body screamed for his caress. *"Yes!"*

"Wonderful! Then I promise a night you will never forget." Quicker than the eye of any digital camera, he hoisted her up and had her stripped of all clothing. His perfect lips found her right nipple and he sucked gently while she gasped happily in his delicious touch. She held her head back, exposing her neck for him. At that point, she realized he had levitated her off the floor and their heads were almost touching the ceiling.

Releasing her nipple, he said, "Don't worry. I could catch you a hundred times before you ever fell to the floor." He quickly kissed the tip of her nose. "Trust me!"

"I do," she breathed. Then she yelled out as he took her.

He chuckled wickedly and swung her around to where her back braced the ceiling. There, he held her at her wrists while he worked her to the point of losing all reason. He smiled to himself. Only a few minutes prior, he had been screwing Nancy. He briefly wondered if Darren was awake yet, and then his focus returned to Mona, who was now the one writhing in ecstasy at his touch. Though Mona was the woman he loved, he was a vampire, and thoroughly enjoyed sex, no matter who he was screwing. Still, he preferred Mona.

"Oh jeeze! Oh shit! Oh jeeze!" It was as though her very insides were going to explode in sheer pleasure. The craving, the yearning, the maddening need for him was unspeakable; she didn't want him to ever stop. "I will never betray you!" she feverishly promised. "Never!"

"I know you won't," he replied and opened his mouth wide and bit hard into her delicate flesh, rapidly drinking her blood, draining her quickly as she reached her climax. He let his pleasure loose and they finished together just as she succumbed. Not dead yet, but unconscious, he swiftly pulled the bed covers back with one hand while he held her with the other, and then laid her on the bed, dressed her and slipped the covers up over her. He heard a wisp of air expel from her lips, her last breath as a human. She was gone.

He stood beside her for several minutes, gazing down on her now porcelain-white skin. She looked like a life-sized China doll. Bending over, he kissed her cheek. "Night, my love. Tomorrow you will rise a vampire – my mate!" He dressed and went to his apartment to make himself a drink and watch television. It was going to be a little while, but she would probably awaken around sunrise. Before that, he would hang some sheets over the few windows in her apartment. Her new vampire skin would be extra sensitive to the rays of the sun. She would have to be very careful for a few days, until she learned how to protect herself from its deadly rays.

Nancy's eyes popped open. Something was wrong. Very wrong. She was having difficulty breathing. She gasped for air. "Da...rren?" Her voice was raspy at its best. "Darren?" She was weak, disoriented, but managed to turn over. The first rays of sunlight had made their way through their bedroom window. Darren was still fast asleep. She reached a hand over to his back, for he was facing away from her. Her throat was dry, hurt like hell. "Darren!" she managed as loud as she could, her voice still hoarse.

"Huh?" he sleepily muttered.

"There's something wrong. I'm sick."

He turned his head slightly. "What?"

She coughed. "I...I can't hardly breathe."

"Say what?" he rolled over then and got a good look at her. "What the hell?" His eyes widened as he realized what he was seeing. "Oh my God! Your neck!"

Puzzled, she said, "My neck?" she reached her hand up. Felt something sticky. She pulled her hand away. Blood! "Oh God! What happened to me?"

Immediately he was out of bed and on his cell phone calling for an ambulance. "My girlfriend's been injured. She's bleeding from her neck," he said to the dispatcher.

Nancy stared up at him, not having a clue what had happened. She mustered up what little strength she had to sit up and pull her legs around to the side of the bed. She wanted to see herself in the dresser mirror, which faced their bed. "Oh Jesus!" she susurrated, seeing the two large, dark holes at the base of her neck, and drying blood everywhere, including her black negligee. "What happened to me?" She suddenly felt faint. Room spinning. She heard Darren yell just as she blacked out.

Doctor Jamison was at the triage station speaking with another doctor when a pretty young woman with golden brown hair and blood all over her black negligee was wheeled by. Her handsome, well-dressed escort, probably her boyfriend, looked vaguely familiar. At first, the doctor thought she'd been in some kind of freak home accident, but just as they were taking her into a nearby room, he saw the two, all-too-familiar, holes in her neck. Then he remembered where and when he'd seen the boyfriend before. "Wait!" he yelled at the medics and held up a forefinger. "I'll take this one!"

Doctor Jamison eyed the worried young man with her. "Clothes hanger?" he quipped cynically, before ordering an African American male nurse by the name of Regan to get her going with a unit of blood.

When the nurse went out, Darren shook his head vigorously. "No! I don't know what happened. We went to bed last night and everything was fine. Then she woke me up this morning having trouble breathing. When I turned over, blood was everywhere and she had those holes in her neck. She passed out while I was calling for an ambulance."

Doctor Jamison's jaw twitched as he seriously considered the evidence. "Anyone else been around?"

"Not that I know of, Doctor." Darren shrugged, every bit as perplexed as the doctor.

"This makes two girls in the past week, you know?"

"I know," Darren replied with a grimace.

The doctor raised suspicious eyes. "And you know both of them."

Darren's head practically vibrated, he was so shook up. "I know what it must look like, doctor, but I swear – I didn't hurt either one of them!"

The nurse returned and set about hooking Nancy up to the IV.

"She's going to need several of those, Regan."

"Yes, doctor."

Doctor Jamison continued to examine Nancy for several more minutes, while Darren stood helplessly by. After a bit, Darren excused himself, said he wanted to call his dad and went on out to the lobby.

Michael was headed out the door when he received the phone call from his frantic son. There was only one other time when had known Darren to be so upset, and that was when Mona had ended up in an all too familiar way. He turned around and looked at his wife, who had stopped in the kitchen doorway, listening. "I'll be right there," he said into the cell phone, but eyes on Margaret. "I'll have Marie hold the fort down and take calls until we get back."

Margaret hurried over to him. "Something's happened to Nancy?"

A sardonic snigger escaped before he answered. "Oddly enough, it appears that whatever or whomever put the holes in Mona's neck has now inflicted the same on Nancy."

Perplexed, she inquired, "But whom? How?"

He shrugged and clasped the doorknob. "Maybe the doctor was right."

"Right about what?"

"I know he was being facetious when he said it, but when Mona was in the hospital, and he was trying to figure out what had happened to her, he remarked that if he didn't know better, he would think she'd been attacked by a vampire."

She was in utter disbelief. "Seriously?"

"Right now, I feel like I just stepped into the Twilight Zone. Again, I hate to say it, but what if he was right?"

"Oh my God! You're serious!"

"Let's hope the doctor was wrong." He turned the knob and opened the door.

"Want me to come with you?"

He hesitated for a moment, looking at her appreciatively. "It's okay. Thoughtful of you to ask. There's probably nothing you can do. However, Darren is your son too, maybe you could stop by later? Check in on her after I get to the office?"

"Yes! Yes! I can do that." She moved up to him and kissed his cheek. "Be careful – Just in case there is any truth to what you just said, although it is all so unbelievable."

With a slight nod, he went on out and closed the door behind him.

"I'll lock it!" she called from her side.

"Thanks," he replied from his.

All was darkness; a deep, frigid well, depths unknown. No sights. No sounds. Something not yet understood reached out, grasping, exploring, searching, for it knew not what. Did it exist? Was there existence? Something shuddered. An awful icy numbness engulfed, shrouded, whatever it was. Out of this black emptiness a slight hint of discomfort made itself known. While black fingers of nothingness webbed out, this seed of aching ignited awareness; only to swiftly transform to hunger. No. Not hunger, a ravenous, insatiable thirst! It thirsted – A desert of parched dryness that demanded quenching. Only there was no relief. It lingered for what seemed forever and then worsened, more overwhelming with each fleeting second. Unbearable!

Mona bolted up in bed. Eyes red as embers. She would have screamed a blood-curdling scream, but her throat was so dry that only gasps of desperation escaped.

Someone stood beside her, offering her something. Was it a straw?

"Drink, Mona!" Gavril said. "This will help the thirst."

She remembered then. They had made love, and he had drunk from her, and then all had turned to blackness.

"Drink," he repeated, carefully slipping the end of the tube between her parched lips.

Her eyes turned to his. He was smiling down at her in such a loving way as she had not seen before. "You are a vampire now, my love. You must drink to gain your strength."

At first, she sucked lightly, not knowing what to expect. A little blood came, just enough for her to taste. It was a little salty, a little thicker than water, but good. No. Not good. Delicious! She grabbed the straw and unit from him and practically gulped the unit down.

All the while, Gavril stood beside her chuckling, amused and happy.

She drained the unit dry and handed it to him. "More!"

He had the second unit ready. ''Here, my sweet. This is the last one."

She grabbed it, practically inhaling the blood.

"It will have to suffice until tonight. Then I will take you out and we will hunt for your first fresh feed."

She rolled her eyes up to his. Little lights came to them, tiny flames of hunger, the hunger for blood. She finished off the second and was instantly out of bed, standing before him. "You sure there's not more? I am *still* thirsty."

Very pleased, he chuckled again. "Tell you what. For now, you may drink of me. It should be enough to get you through until the dark hours, when we can safely go out."

"Drink from you?"

"Yes! We can do that. Drink from one another. It helps quench the thirst and, I might add, it is kind of erotic, as you will see.

Vampire mates do it all the time. Share their blood. It will give you a chance to try out your fangs."

An impish grin spread across her lips. "Fangs? I now have *fangs?"*

"Yes, my sweet. All vampires have fangs. Blood is our natural sustenance. For that, fangs are most helpful."

Her fingers went to her mouth. Her mouth did feel different, and it wasn't just from the dryness that had been there. Underneath her upper lip, felt swollen on both sides. She stuck her finger in her mouth and felt the bumps, one on each side. "Wow!" she said. "How do they work, though? How do I get them to come down?"

He laughed heartily. "Do not worry your pretty head about it. They will protrude automatically when you go to bite into flesh. A natural response such as salivating."

"Can I bite you now?"

He quickly pulled his black turtleneck collar down to the side, exposing his neck, and leaned his head sideways. "Be my guest."

Just staring at the offered treat in anticipation did it. Her fangs sprout forth as promised.

Darren had pulled a chair up by Nancy's bed and sat there watching her labored breathing. She was so white! So pale! Even with a transfusion going now, she didn't appear to be gaining any strength or color. He glanced at his watch. It had only been going about fifteen minutes. He leaned over, elbows on his thighs, hands rubbing his face. "God!" he susurrated, wondering if he had, somehow, brought this on by some weird karma, because of the things he had done. As self-centered and conceited as Nancy was, she didn't deserve this. Not this! He was terrified she wasn't going to make it. As ill as Mona had been, Nancy was worse. She appeared whiter, if that were possible? What's more, her struggle to hang onto life seemed more profound. He sat up straight then, as he heard footsteps coming in the door – his dad. "Oh God! So glad you're here, Dad."

Michael moved up to Nancy's bedside and stood in front of Darren. He blew out air. "I hate to say it, but she looks even worse than Mona did."

"I know. Just what I was thinking."

A sudden knock on the door got their attention. Doctor Jamison burst in and closed the door behind him. He eased down on the bottom end of Nancy's bed. He sat his clipboard aside and eyed the two worried men waiting for some kind of answers. "I thought of calling the police."

"I wondered about that," Michael admitted, glancing briefly at his son before returning his attention back to the doctor. "In fact, I was surprised there wasn't an officer standing outside the door here."

"Have to admit, it is beyond weird and *very* suspicious." The doctor addressed Darren. "I don't … can't… say who or *what* is behind this, as I stated before, when the other girl was in here: This is something totally unknown to me. Before the other girl, I'd never seen wounds like this. Logically, I should report this to the police. Only I have the distinct feeling that the police would be useless in helping solve these… incidences." His stare went from Michael to Darren and back to Michael. "I need your help here. Do either of you have any idea at all what could have happened to these two young women?"

Michael looked over at his son, who appeared to want to speak but also seemed afraid to. "Darren, you want to tell the doctor anything?"

Doctor Jamison eyed Darren curiously. "Is there something?"

"I don't like this new neighbor of Mona's," Darren admitted.

"He's a neighbor of the other girl?"

"Yes! He is," Darren admitted.

"Does he know Nancy?"

"I can't be sure. He may. I do know that he seems to really like Mona – You see, Mona and I used to live together in the apartment where she lives now. I moved out. Then this new neighbor moved in almost immediately after. He's the one who gives me the willies when I'm around him."

"Anything unusual about him, other than the way he makes you feel?"

Michael spoke, "He's a foreigner."

"Okay. That's something. Wouldn't happen to know where he's from, would you?"

"Does that make a difference?" Darren asked.

"Maybe. Maybe not. But the more we know the better."

"I believe he's from Romania," Michael offered. "At least, that's what Mona told me."

The doctor seemed to find that slightly amusing, letting out a cryptic chuckle.

"What?" Darren asked, shifting around in his chair. "Why is that so funny?"

"You remember my flippant reference to a vampire being the cause of Mona's wounds?"

"Yes. What about it?"

Michael answered for Darren. "Romania is where Dracula was from, Darren."

Darren's brow wrinkled slightly in a puzzled frown, his mouth gaped as though to speak, but he said nothing, and then his stare went to the doctor. "Ahhh…"

"I realize I could lose my license to practice over something like this, but I have no other explanation for the wounds on both of these young women. Not only their wounds, but for the extreme loss of blood from both. After the other girl was in here, I couldn't put it out of my mind. I went home and did a lot of research on vampires." He stretched his neck around to the right and then to the left, relieving kinks. "I'll be honest with you. If anyone asks, I will deny that I ever even mentioned such a possibility all the way to my grave. Don't want to lose my practice here. If more cases like this come in and are brought to my attention, then I will do my damdest to get other doctors involved, but not tell them what I'm thinking. That way, if they come up with the same possibility, maybe we won't be laughed out of the hospital and out of our licenses."

"I can certainly understand that," Michael said.

Darren held his hands out to his sides. "If it is a... vampire," he whispered, "then what can we do about it?"

"Wooden stakes," the doctor cryptically remarked. He shook his head apologetically. "Sorry. This hasn't exactly put me in a good mood. To answer your question: I can't say for sure. We need to know beyond any doubt, if that is, indeed, what we are dealing with here. So, I trust you two gentlemen will work with me on this. Can you find out more about this new neighbor?"

"He's pretty spooky," Darren said without hesitation.

"If there is a real life vampire at work here, perhaps this spooky neighbor is the one?" Doctor Jamison stood and picked up his clipboard. His gaze went to Nancy. "Her color's looking better. I wasn't sure we could save her when you brought her in." He turned to Darren. "Hopefully, she'll make it." He sighed heavily and put on an optimistic face. "I have more patients to attend to, but I'll be back before my shift ends... And besides the nurses keeping vigilance, there is a young intern by the name of Doctor Coligado coming in to take over for me later. Of course, he doesn't know what crazy things I am thinking here, but I did tell him that this is a special case, to keep his eyes and ears open and not to hesitate to call me, should anything come up, unusual or otherwise."

"Thank you, Doctor Jamison," Darren said.

"Save the thanks for when she's out of the woods." With that, he flashed them a hopeful smile and made a swift exit.

Sated for the moment from the two units of blood and quenching the rest of her thirst on Gavril, Mona moved slowly to the window to peek out.

"Careful, my love," Gavril warned. "You are a vampire now. I believe it is overcast, but still take heed."

Bobbing her head slightly, indicating that she understood, she ever so tentatively grasped the edges of the sheet and heavy dark green drape that Gavril had put up, and pulled them back marginally. It only took a nanosecond and she jumped back.

"Ouch!" Brow furrowed, her glance turned to Gavril. "I thought we could look out when it's cloudy?"

"You can. I didn't say it wouldn't sting a little."

"That's right. You didn't." She thought about it a minute.

"Go ahead. Try again. What little burning you will feel won't last. We heal rather quickly."

"Okay." Letting out a little sigh, she turned back to the window. This time, she stood there in spite of the slight stinging. She let out another, more mournful sigh.

"Regrets?"

"Just one. I wish I had gone to see Rick Harrison before I let you turn me."

"You should have said something, my sweet." He stepped forward and stood by her, gazing down at the busy street below.

"It's my fault. I was so focused on what was going to happen to me that I simply forgot."

"Is there any particular thing you wanted to speak to him about?"

"I don't really remember. I just feel that he is innocent and needs all the help he can get."

He nuzzled his nose in her hair, relishing its sweet perfume. "One of the things I love so much about you, my sweet – your thoughtfulness."

She faced him and immediately read that glint in his black eyes and forgot all about Rick Harrison. She pounced on him like a cat, kissing him instantly. The passion, the hunger, the need was so immediately profound. She wasn't used to such amazing arousal coming on so instantaneously.

In a blur, they were on the ceiling and having wild, unbridled sex. She bit hard into his shoulder, and he bit her back. She squealed in delight. He laughed. They rolled over and over across the ceiling and back again, all the while making love in a whirlwind of passion.

"I can't stand it!" she blurted. "I have never wanted anyone the way I want you!"

"Your desires are greatly heightened now that you are a vampire, Mona," he breathlessly managed.

She gasped and wrapped her arms and legs around him as tightly as she could while he gave her want she wanted. Then she cried out in erotic pleasure as they came together. They stayed there on the ceiling for several minutes while they cooled down. After a bit, she broke into a huge grin.

"What, my love?" he asked, eyeing her fondly.

"Sex was beyond awesome with you before you turned me. But this! Shit! If I had known sex was going to be like *this* – what we just had – I wouldn't have hesitated to have you turn me. Gads!"

He chuckled from his throat. ""Glad you like, my darling." He glanced down at the floor. "Shall we return to earth?"

Eyes smiling, she replied, "Of course." At once they both stood on the living room floor.

"Now… What about Rick Harrison? Do you still want to go see him?"

"I can't, can I?"

"Any reason we can't go after dark?"

"I believe they have rules on visitation times."

"But you work for a lawyer. Can't you get in to see him, regardless?"

She bit on her bottom lip, considering his words. "Maybe. I really should let Michael know, but I don't want him to know."

"No reason you can't try."

"You're right," she replied, holding her head back and staring into his resplendent eyes. "No reason I can't try."

"That's my girl." He smiled, greatly pleased with his new mate.

Her expression changed to a devilish grin.

"What, dear?"

"Let's do it again."

"Make love?"

"Yes!"

"Ah! My sweet, you are truly a vampire now. There are only two things we ever really need or want – blood and sex." He laughed loudly and grabbed her. Soon they were at it again. This time, in the floor.

Michael was stunned when he walked into his office shortly after one and Marie, who was sitting at his desk, told him that Mona had phoned in and said she wouldn't be coming into work.

"Did she say why?"

"No, Mr. Graves. Just to tell you she couldn't make it today."

He barked an incredulous laugh. This was so unlike her. He was having great difficulty in believing she would do such a thing to him. "No explanations. No reasons given. That's it?"

Marie's face held pity for Michael at that moment. "I know. It's not like her at all. I'm sorry, Mr. Graves."

"Did she sound sick? Or anxious at all?"

"No, sir. She sounded fine. In fact…"

"In fact, what?"

"I had the feeling she was kind of laughing at me… Like she found something funny."

"Say what?"

"Laughing, sir."

He spun on his heels and hung his hat on the rack in the corner of the room, and then turned back to face Marie. "Well, I guess we'll have to make the most of it. Think you can handle it?"

"I'll do my best, sir."

"All right. We have a lot to do. Darren won't be coming in either. Nancy's in the hospital."

"I know, sir. Your message this morning. Why I am here at your desk… Is it serious?"

"Sort of. The doctor thinks she'll pull out of it though."

It was apparent she wanted to know more, but she didn't probe. "That's good."

He let out a long sigh. "Guess we'd better get to work."

"Right, sir. There are several phone calls you need to return."

"Okay. Get the first one on the line for me."

"Right, sir." She ran off into Mona's office to make the call for him.

A little after seven p.m. there was a knock on Gloria's front door. "Hmmm…" she wondered who in the world it could be, but was happily surprised when she saw her daughter and the very handsome Count Gavril Conta standing there. "Mona! You look absolutely radiant!" she stated as she opened the door for them to enter. "Please come on in!"

The couple smiled secretively to one another and stepped inside.

Thrilled by the surprise visit and in seeing Mona looking so well, Gloria was beside herself. "Can I get you something? Coffee? Tea? Cookies? Made a small batch of chocolate chip today. Don't make very many at a time with just myself here to eat them. Store half the dough in the freezer until I want more."

Mona's smile was full of fondness for her mother, but there was something else there too, something enigmatic. "We're fine, Mom. Not hungry."

"That we are… fine, that is," Gavril assured her. "Why don't you just sit down?"

Touching her hand to her chest, she nodded and sat down in her recliner. "I can't get over how good you look, Mona. Last time I saw you, you were just getting well from… whatever it was."

"I feel good too."

"Yes. She's doing very well," Gavril agreed. He winked at his mate and then smiled pleasantly at Gloria.

"What's going on? Mona doesn't usually pay me surprise visits. Usually calls first."

"That's just it. We wanted to surprise you, Mom."

"And a pleasant surprise it is." Her eyes turned to the handsome Gavril and then back to her daughter.

"I'll get to it, Mom. Gavril has invited me to take a trip with him to Europe."

Mouth instantly agape, it took Gloria a moment to ingest what her daughter said. "Europe?"

"Yes!" Gavril explained. "I am from Romania. I want Mona to see where I grew up."

"Why that's great." Addressing her daughter then, "You're just visiting right? Not moving there?" Turning apologetically to Gavril. "It's so far! There is no way I could afford to come visit there."

"Not to worry, Gloria. I can call you Gloria, can't I?"

"Of course."

"It's just for a visit. Actually, I have some business matters to tie up there. Have a lot of property in Transylvania."

"Transylvania? You mean where Bram Stoker's Dracula was from?"

An amused but subdued laugh worked its way up in Gavril's throat. "So, you are familiar with my ancestor."

Her eyes widened. "Your… Your ancestor?"

He chuckled again. "Yes. Actually, I am a distant cousin of the real Dracula."

"Oh my gosh!" She couldn't have been more thrilled. "I have absolutely loved the stories of Dracula all my life. Now you're telling me you are a relative to the real Dracula?"

"That I am. In fact, I want to show Mona what was once Bran Castle. However, not to be confused with the true Dracula castle, Poenari, located on the Arges River." He grinned as though proud of himself and said, "Which I have done my best to duplicate. My home, when I'm not traveling around the rest of the world."

"Goodness! How exciting!"

Mona smiled secretively at her vampire lover. He was making her mother very happy.

"Perhaps someday in the not too far future, I will pay your way over."

Her eyes went to Mona and back to Gavril. "Seriously? Oh my gosh! This is so unbelievable!"

"I would invite you this time, but Mona and I want some 'special' time together."

"Of course, I understand."

"You see," he said, grinning good-naturedly, "I plan on asking Mona to be my wife."

This was a surprise to Mona. She snapped her head around. "What?"

"Did you not think I would want to marry you, my love?'

Now she was the one with the gaping mouth.

He guffawed and quickly pulled a ring out of his blazer pocket, a ring with a huge diamond. "Mona, will you be my wife?"

Gloria screamed excitedly. One would have thought he'd asked for her hand in marriage.

"Shit!" Mona exclaimed, eyes tearing. "I had no idea you were going to propose."

"Of course, you didn't. I wanted to surprise you." He kissed her sweetly and then pulled away, smiling at Gloria, who was practically glowing from excitement.

"Let me see it," she said, reaching out for Mona's hand.

Mona placed her fingertips in her mother's open palm.

"I do not believe I've ever seen a diamond that big... Not ever!

"I aim to please."

"I take it you are well-off. I know of no one who could afford a rock that big."

"It's not the size so much or what it costs, but the thought behind it. Yes. I love your daughter, and I do have wealth untold. Even if I didn't, I would want only the best for my bride."

Mona took back her hand then, examining the ring herself. "This is so beautiful!" Her eyes danced happily as she gazed at Gavril.

"Well? Do I get a yes?"

She laughed at herself; hand going to her mouth. "Yes! Yes! I will marry you!" She threw her arms around his neck.

"I thought you'd never say it." They sealed it with a kiss.

Gloria stood. "This calls for a celebration. Will you two please join me in a glass of wine?"

"Most assuredly," Gavril replied, slowly pulling away from Mona.

Gloria went to get the wine and glasses.

Michael dropped by the hospital before going on home for the day. As he entered Nancy's room, Darren was sitting where he had left him earlier that day. Nancy had more color but was asleep.

"She ever wake up?" Michael inquired, taking the end of the bed to sit.

"A couple of times. One of the nurses got her to eat some chicken soup, but she went right back to sleep afterwards."

"Darren, I know you've had a rough day, but there's something I have wanted to ask you for a while now."

"Oh? What's that?"

"You wouldn't remember what you were doing August sixteenth, would you?"

"What? What does that have to do with anything?" Clearly, he was puzzled.

"Not sure that it does. Off hand, I thought you were with Mona that evening, but when I asked her, she said you had gone somewhere without her."

"I don't know, Dad." He rubbed his brow and dropped down his hand. "Can't it wait? Seems a little trivial right now… under the circumstances." He indicated with a nod to Nancy.

Michael laid a hand on his son's shoulder. "You're right, son. Not the time to ask." He glanced at his watch and flashed an insignificant smile. "Well, unless you need me for something, I'm going to head on home now. Your mother is actually cooking a fried chicken dinner this evening. She told me to invite you."

"Chicken sounds good. Only I don't know if I should leave Nancy."

A burly male nurse walked in just then. He had heard. "Go ahead and get something to eat. We're keeping a close watch on this young lady here," he said as he checked all the monitors.

"All right." Darren stood. "I think I will."

"Want to ride with me? I can bring you back."

"That's okay, Dad. I'll take my car. I want to run by the house and grab a few things before I come back."

"Okay, son."

Taking a quick glance at the still sleeping Nancy, he followed his dad on out the door.

Chapter Nine:

Though it was a little more than out of the way and growing late, Darren drove by the Starbucks anyway, hoping the little strawberry blonde had stayed after school and then gone by to grab a mocha, as she often did, before heading home. No such luck, though. No sign of her inside or on the sidewalk outside. "Shit! What am I doing?" he asked himself. Then he remembered his dad asking him as to his whereabouts on August sixteenth. The date wanted to ring a bell, but he couldn't quite remember. Was it someone's birthday he should remember? A silly anniversary of some kind? What? What could be so important that his dad would bother to ask when Nancy was in the hospital, seriously ill?

He pulled in the guests parking at the apartment complex and shut off his engine. His thoughts strayed back to the young girl. That was when it hit him – August the sixteenth was the day he raped the Gilbert girl. "Oh my God!" his hands flew to his face. His dad suspected! After all this time, his dad had come across something. But what? It was a sure thing that Mona had been going through the files. "Oh Jesus! Oh damn!" He sat there several minutes, fighting the panic that wanted to rise. "Got to get a hold of myself. Got to! Dad can't know for sure. He's only putting two and two together. Just because I wasn't with Mona, doesn't mean I was with Lee Gilbert." He carried a small bottle of Tylenol in his pocket. He popped a couple in his mouth, hoping it would, somehow, aid him in calming down. He picked up a half-full bottle of water that was in the holder by his seat and drank that down. "Okay," he told himself. "Just act normal. If he asks again, tell him you don't remember for sure, but you think you were out with some of your buddies that evening. After all, it was a while back." Telling himself that, he got out of his car, locked it and headed on up to his parents' apartment.

Rick Harrison was a little more than surprised to not only have but be allowed a visitor so late in the evening. Mona Sims, all decked out in a black satin blouse, black leather slacks and silver, hoop earrings – not exactly the conservative business attire he was accustomed to seeing her in – waited for him at the table as the jailer brought him in. He stared at her. It wasn't just her attire that was different. There was something else about her that was too. She was prettier than he remembered, and her eyes were all sparkly and fiery. If he hadn't known better, he would have thought her to be someone else.

"What do I owe this pleasure?" he asked as he took a chair opposite her at the table. He glanced back at the guard stepping out the door. After the door closed, he turned back around in his seat.

"I just wanted to see you before I left."

Puzzled, he tilted his head back. "I don't understand. You're leaving? What does that have to do with me?"

"Just that I have been, and still am, interested in your case. I know Michael, Mr. Graves, my former employer – although he isn't aware of it yet – is very interested in proving your innocence."

"I hate to see you go, Ms. Sims, but I'm afraid I still don't understand."

"Let's put it this way – I know you're innocent."

"You do? How?"

"Can't tell you. I will tell you, however, that you will be set free soon."

He cleared his throat. "I sure hope you're right. Only I don't see how. From my perspective, things don't look too good. What do you know that I don't?"

"Just trust me, Mr. Harrison." She scooted back in her chair and stood. "I just wanted to let you know that it would all be over soon."

He held out his hands to his sides in gesture. "Well, thank you! And thanks for coming by to see me."

"My pleasure."

He craned his head around to watch her as she went to walk out of the room. Something was really different with her!

"Ah…" He stood.

"Yes?" She spun back around.

"You said your boss didn't know you weren't working for him anymore… and that you're leaving. Can I ask where you're going?"

"Sure. Romania. Going with my fiancée."

"Romania, huh?" He grinned kiddingly, "You mean where Dracula hailed from?"

Her eyes sparkled brilliantly. "One and the same. You have a good life, Mr. Harrison."

"You too. And thank you!"

"You just take care of yourself and your daughters when you get out."

"I will certainly do that."

She went through the door and disappeared to the right.

He wasn't sure why, but he knew she had told the truth. There was just something about her, something he couldn't put his finger on. Still, he had no doubts that he would be out soon. The guard came in for him then and he returned to his cell.

Darren was about to slip into his raincoat when there was a knock on his parent's door. He glanced over to his mom and dad relaxing on the sofa. "Expecting company?"

Margaret sat forward. "No, Son."

"I wasn't expecting anyone," Michael replied.

Margaret lit a cigarette and leaned back. "Since you're on your way out, want to get if for us?"

"Sure. Why not?" He shrugged the rest of the way into his coat and opened the door. "Oh!" he said, startled. For Mona and Gavril stood there, smiling mysteriously.

"Evening," Gavril said, flashing very white teeth.

"Who is it?" Michael asked, leaning forward, trying to see around his son.

Darren stepped aside, frowning confusedly. "It's… Mona, Dad."

"Are you going to invite us in?" Mona asked.

Michael stood and went to the door. "Of course. Come on in." His attention went to Mona first. He thought: *Wow! Something's changed about her. She's always been beautiful, but I never noticed her looking so hot before!* "I have a bone to pick with you, Mona. You didn't come to the office today."

She and Gavril stepped in and she turned to face Michael. "I really am sorry about that. I know it wasn't very nice of me. I've come to apologize. I really never meant to do that to you."

Instantly, he had to fight off arousal from just looking into her eyes. *Shit!* He turned to Gavril. There was something about the man that gave him the chills. He looked back at Mona and realized then, that in spite of the arousal he was trying very hard to fight against, he was getting similar, chilling vibes from her, as well. He did his best to ward off the powerful urges to jump her bones and recoil at the same time. "There's something different about you. What is it? You change your hair?"

"Just my plans." Her ambiguous smile told him that she knew exactly what he was thinking.

Gavril spoke, "Forgive me, Michael. I have to tell you that Mona not coming in today was my fault. You see… I asked her to marry me."

"Oh?" Michael couldn't help hide some of the hurt he felt at that moment, even though he had given up on his and Mona's being together, but now he was secretly thinking that maybe it was a good thing.

"And I'm happy to say that she accepted."

"Kind of sudden, isn't it?" he spoke before thinking it through.

There was a flash of anger in Gavril's eyes, but then it vanished, and he smiled politely. "Yes. You're so right. It is a bit sudden." He put an arm around Mona. "However, I need to go home for a little while, and I didn't want to take a chance on losing Mona to someone else," he raised a knowing eyebrow in Michael's direction, "while away. So, I told her how I felt and, to my surprise, she said yes."

Michael cleared his throat as he stared at Mona. He went through the gamut of emotions – hurt, anger, sense of betrayal and, compounding it all, fear. No. Not fear – Terror! What he saw in Mona's eyes, now, besides seduction, scared the hell out of him. She was not the same Mona he had fallen in love with. Something in her had changed. Changed drastically. "I understand," he said, but he really didn't. He didn't understand at all.

Margaret stood and came over to her husband immediately. "This calls for a celebratory drink, don't you think, Michael?" Her glance was that of a wife who knew her husband well.

Michael cleared his throat. "Yes! Definitely. You two will have a drink with us, won't you?"

"I have to get to the hospital," Darren said.

"Hospital?" Gavril inquired, feigning ignorance to the matter.

Darren observed him with caution. "Yes! Nancy. Nancy was injured."

"Nancy?" Mona said innocently, even though Gavril had confessed his little indiscretion to her, for they had vowed to be perfectly honest with one another. "What happened?"

"It seems that somehow she managed to lose a lot of blood." His stare went to Gavril.

Gavril's brow rose marginally. "So sorry to hear that. Will she be all right?"

"It was questionable, at first. However, the doctors gave her several units of blood, and she seems to be coming along okay now."

"That's good," Mona said. She looked up at Gavril. "Maybe we should stop by to see her?"

Before Gavril could answer, Darren blurted, "It's not necessary. Besides, the doctor wants her to get as much rest as possible. She's been sleeping a lot. I'm going to go home and grab a few things and go stay the night with her."

"Very commendable of you," Gavril said, black eyes shining mysteriously.

"Well, I'm out of here." He gave a nod to his folks and went out the door, closing it behind him.

Michael held his gaze on Gavril. "Can we get you two those drinks?"

"For sure." He winked at Mona and they followed Michael and Margaret over to the little bar.

While they enjoyed their drinks, Gavril explained to Michael again that Mona's not coming in was his fault. "I also apologize for her not calling, as well. She meant to, but I sidetracked her," he said with a mischievous grin, "and we seemed to have forgotten about it. That is, until a little bit ago. Again, my apologies."

"I do feel awful, Michael. You've been such a terrific boss to work for."

"Been?" He gesticulated with his outstretched hand. "I take it that you're not coming in anymore?"

She shared a glance with Gavril, who nodded for her to answer. "I can't."

"Oh?" He glanced at his wife and then back to Mona. He was actually relieved that she wasn't coming back to work. Not the way she was now. "I have to admit I wasn't happy about you standing us up today. However, your exemplary performance for the rest of the time you've been with us would allow me to forgive you this one discretion."

Her eyes misted over. "That is so sweet of you. But—."

"We're leaving for Romania in the morning," Gavril answered for her.

"Oh! Romania! Well…"

Margaret took her husband's elbow in a show of support. "How exciting! I've always wanted to travel to Romania."

"Interesting," Gavril noted.

Michael looked down at his wife in surprise. "You never told me."

"I know. I have often thought it might be someplace I'd like to see. You know… the old castles, and such."

"I have a home there," Gavril said. "A castle, in fact. You and Michael would be most welcome. That is, if we happen to be there when you want to come. For now, I'm just taking Mona on a visit. However, if she really likes it, we may move back there eventually."

Gavril and Mona finished off their drinks and Margaret offered them another.

Gavril checked the time on his watch. "Thank you, but we need to get going. Need to pack and all that."

Michael looked at Mona and managed a smile. "We'll miss you, Mona." He would. But it would be the old Mona he would miss. In fact, he already missed her. Yet, he had the distinct feeling that she wasn't ever coming back. No. The old Mona was gone. Now, before him was a new Mona, and not one he was sure he wanted to know any better. *Vampire,* stuck in his mind.

She and Gavril stood from where they'd been sitting at the bar. "I will miss you too, Michael." She hugged him, and then Margaret.

Margaret said, "Well, you two come to see us, if you come back this way."

"For sure," Gavril said and took Margaret's hand, kissing it in a gentlemanly manner. "We will, Mrs. Graves." Then, standing straight, he took Mona's arm and they went to the door.

Michael opened it for them. They bid each other goodbye and Gavril and Mona left.

Darren knew he should go straight to the hospital, but he felt compelled to drive by Starbucks again. He glanced inside, not really expecting to see the pretty strawberry blonde, but couldn't really believe his eyes when he saw her in there, waiting in line for a coffee. He found the nearest open space along the curb, swung his car in and parked. He thought about it a moment. He only came in the Starbucks occasionally, but he knew the girl was in there almost daily. He wore glasses part of the time, but really mostly needed them for reading. As an added precaution, he grabbed his eyeglass case out of his glove compartment and slipped them on, and then jumped out, locked the car and dashed into Starbucks.

She turned to look just as walked in. He smiled warmly and went up to her. "What a pleasant surprise to see you here this time of an evening," he said.

She didn't recognize him at first. "Excuse me?"

"Oh! The glasses." He pointed a finger to his face. "Don't wear them all the time."

"Oh! Yeah! I recognize you now."

"Awesome."

She touched a hand to her chest. "We're having a school dance this weekend, and I'm on the decorating committee. We just finished our meeting. Decided I wanted something hot, since it is chilly outside. Ordered a mocha, of course."

"Of course," he replied. Then the barista asked him what he wanted. He told her that he wanted what the young lady ordered.

The barista handed the girl's drink over.

She took it and smiled pleasantly at Darren. She seemed to be pondering something, and then suddenly said, "Want to join me when you get yours?"

"Why thank you! I'd like that." He winked and recognized the little light of hope in her pretty eyes. She was flattered that a handsome, older man would even be interested in her. He was interested all right. Couldn't wait to get her alone. He shoved that tiny voice of conscience back into his subconscious; the voice of reason, the voice of integrity, the voice of just plain old common sense. He just couldn't help himself. Had to have her. Had to! Already, he was undressing her in his mind.

He forgot all about Nancy lying in the hospital, having been so close to death. He forgot Mona, the girl he had been so sorry he dumped so easily. None of that mattered to him at that moment. The desire to take this lovely young girl was overwhelming. The simple thought of it thrilled him beyond measure.

They sat there talking for a good half hour before she finally glanced at her phone. "Goodness! It's eight o'clock! I have homework!" She jumped up. "Hope I didn't miss my bus!"

"Not to worry," he said and stood with her. "My car's right down the street. Let me take you home."

"Oh?" she responded with surprise. "You sure you don't mind?"

"Absolutely not."

"I don't even know your name."

"Carl. Carl Sanderson," he lied.

"I'm Allison Hays," she said with a big smile.

"Okay, Allison. Let me give you a lift." He glanced at the barista, who was watching them with mild interest. He didn't want problems. Didn't want her to see them leave together.

"I really appreciate you doing this, Carl."

"Not a problem. Tell you what. My car's about a half a block away. Let me run on out and start it up. I'll drive around the block. You come on out in a couple of minutes. Can't miss it. It's a red Porsche."

"Sure. Can I take a quick trip to the little girl's room?"

Perfect, he thought. "Go right ahead. It will probably take me a minute to get through all the traffic anyway." He headed on out the door, while she went to the bathroom.

The traffic was so heavy and the rain pouring down so hard that it took Darren almost five minutes to get back around to pick Allison up. She was waiting there, though, smiling a very happy and friendly smile. A thrill shot through him as he thought about what he was going to do to her. He leaned across the front seat and opened the door for her, while she dashed across and jumped inside, fastening her seat belt.

"You're all wet," he said, apologetically. "I was hoping to get here faster."

"That's all right," she said. "I was under the canopy, but the wind was still blowing the rain in my face."

Reaching to the dash, he turned the heat up and winked. "That should have you dried off by the time I get you home."

"Yes. It should. Thanks."

Realizing he had a woody, he quickly pulled his raincoat over himself to conceal it. Then, turning his head towards her, he asked for her address. Turned out, she lived only ten blocks away. Deliberately, he made a wrong turn.

"Wrong way!" she said, smiling still, not sensing yet that she was in danger. "The next block over."

"Oh! Sorry." He drove around the corner, leading her to think he was still taking her home, but then he suddenly swung into an alley, driving down it kind of fast.

"What are you doing?" she asked puzzled now. "You're still heading the wrong way."

"Not to worry," he feigned a smile. "Just need to make a quick stop. That all right with you?"

Not looking so certain but afraid to say otherwise, she said, "Yes... Sure."

He knew just the place, an old abandoned warehouse. It was where he had taken Trisha Landsbury five years prior. He turned down another alley and drove right into an open garage door. There, he jumped out, hitting a switch on the side and closed the door, and then ran around to the other side, opening her door. "Come on. This won't take long."

Suspicion growing, she was worried. "Can't I just wait here in the car?"

"Nah. You don't want to do that. Come on. Get out."

Looking downcast, she fidgeted with her fingers in her lap. "I'd really rather not."

His patience had grown thin. It was do it now or never. "I said... get out!"

No doubt now that his intentions weren't good, she jumped out of the car but stood back from him.

"Better." He grabbed her arm. "It's this way."

She yanked her arm back and yelled, "I don't want to go with you!" She took off running, desperately looking for a way out of the garage; she finally found a door, pushed it open and disappeared into the thrumming rain.

He caught sight of her just before she disappeared out the door. "Dammit!" He couldn't let her get away. He charged out after her, looking to the left first, where he thought she had gone. Didn't see her. He spun around to the right. Still didn't see her. "Shi-it!" he hissed. There were buildings on each side of the abandoned garage.

He ran to the left and glanced between the buildings there. No sign of her. His breathing increased, panic escalating. Chances of her finding help before he could cover his tracks were marginal now. "Jesus!" He ran back the other way and checked between the buildings there. He saw her. At least, that was what he thought, until she was suddenly in his face – Mona!

Her eyes were red as coals. "Looking for someone, Darren? A young girl perhaps?"

"What the fuck?" That was when, behind her a few feet away, he saw Gavril with Allison. She was pointing an accusing finger at Darren.

Mona said, "Go ahead and get her out of here, Gavril. I'll take care of Darren."

"Yes, my love," he said, and then, holding the girl's hand, they vanished into thin air.

Mona slammed him against the outside wall of the garage, mouth open wide and two very sharp – looked like fangs – protruded from her mouth.

Darren screamed just as she sunk her fangs deep into the fold of his neck. "Oh God!" he cried. "Oh God!"

She suddenly released him and let him drop to the ground.

"Please don't kill me, Mona… Whatever or whoever you are?"

Her smile was devilish and her eyes still shown an unworldly radiance as she spoke. "I am willing to make a deal with you."

He sat there cowering at her feet. "Huh? A deal? What kind of a deal?"

"You want me to drink every ounce of blood from your miserable body? Or do you want to live?"

"What?"

"You heard me."

"I want to live! I want to live!"

"Okay," she said, retracting her fangs. "Turn yourself in."

"No!"

The fangs appeared again.

"Oh shit! Wait! Okay! I'll turn myself in!"

"Promise?"

"...Promise. Oh dear Jesus... Yes! I'm sorry. I don't really want to hurt anyone. I just can't seem to help myself."

"Then confess. You'll spend some time in jail... prison, probably, but you should get the psychiatric help you need."

"Okay. I'll do whatever you say. Just don't kill me. Please!"

"As long as you keep your promise, I won't."

" Thank you!" he began crying like a baby. "Thank you!"

Gavril suddenly appeared alone. "The girl is safe at home now."

"Good," Mona said. "Did you compel her?"

"Yes!" he said, eyeing Darren intently, as though he might want to sample his blood too. "She won't remember a thing. Only that she stayed after school and got caught in a downpour waiting for the bus. A friend came along and took her home."

"Oh thank you!" Darren said, pulling himself up and standing.

Mona slammed him against the wall again. "Not so quick."

"I don't understand?"

Gavril spoke, "You don't need to confess about Allison. After all, though you definitely intended to, you didn't rape her. However, you have to confess to raping the other two girls."

"No... No... No..."

At once, both vampires were at his sides, baring their fangs, their hot breath tickling his neck.

"I'll do it!" he yelled. "I'll confess!"

"To your father first," Mona said.

Darren was taken aback by that. "My... My father? I... I... I..."

"Yes!" Mona hissed. "We intend to let you stay with Nancy tonight. However, in the morning, you must turn yourself into your father."

"That or die," Gavril reminded him.

He considered the alternative. "Okay." His head bobbed as though it were on a coil. "Okay. I'll do it."

"Damn right, you will," Gavril stated. "Soon as Nancy is awake in the morning, you have to call your dad, if he isn't already there, and tell him."

"Okay! I'll do it! Promise!"

"Wise decision."

"You can go now," Mona informed him. "But just know this; we will know if you deviate from your promise at all. If you do, we *will* kill you!"

"I won't deviate. I'll do as you say."

"Good. Glad we have an understanding." Gavril put his arm around Mona. "Shall we, my love?"

"Yes. I'm hungry."

Gavril told Darren to enjoy the rest of his evening, and then he and Mona vanished.

Doctor Jamison and several nurses were in Nancy's room when Darren finally arrived. Nurse Regan was there, wheeling out some machinery on a cart. The doctor was taking Nancy's pulse. Done, he eased Nancy's wrist down. That was when Darren realized Nancy was awake. He felt instant relief. Only he was puzzled by all the attention she was receiving. Speaking to Doctor Jamison, he asked, "Is Nancy okay?"

Nancy smiled and replied for him. "Yes! I feel much better, Darren."

Doctor Jamison glanced askance at Darren. "I need to speak with you." He took hold of Darren's upper arm and ushered him out into the hall, closing the door behind them.

"What is it?" he asked, knowing he wasn't sure if he wanted to know.

"Weird… Whatever the cause of hers and the other woman's malady… I'll be honest. Again, never saw anything like it."

"What, Doctor Jamison? What?"

"She flat lined about half an hour ago. We thought we had lost her for sure. We even called the time of death and were ready to have her shipped downstairs, when all of a sudden she gasped in air and her eyes popped open. Startled the crap out of all of us."

"What? You mean to tell me you thought she was dead?"

"Exactly what I'm telling you. That was odd in itself, even though I have seen it happen before. What is really strange about it, though, is she appears fine now. In fact, her vitals are strong. It is almost as though she was never ill."

"That is weird. But it is good, isn't it?"

"Definitely. Still, due to the severity of how she was only an hour ago, I have no intentions of releasing her yet. I want to keep her here for another twenty-four hours for observation. And, between you and me, just out of plain old curiosity."

"I understand. I think. That's good. I want to know beyond any doubt that she is okay when she leaves here."

"Good. I want that too."

Doctor Jamison gave Darren a couple of hearty slaps on his arm. "You take care. I'll see you tomorrow."

Darren bobbed his head. He wasn't so sure he would see the doctor again, but he was glad that Nancy was okay. The rest of the nurses walked out after the doctor, and then Darren went on in and sat down by Nancy's bedside. He touched her cheek lovingly. "So glad you're going to be okay."

She reflected his smile. "Me too. Only, I really am thirsty. Can you hand me my water glass?"

He filled the glass for her from the pitcher that sat on her tray and handed it over. She sat up and took it, drinking the water down quickly. She handed the glass back.

"Better now?" He returned the glass to the tray.

"A little... But..."

"But what, honey?"

"I'm craving something. Not sure what though."

"Want me to see if they can send you something up from the kitchen?"

"Yes! Would you please?"

"Anything in particular?"

She thought about it. "Meat. See if they have any steak... rare."

"I'll do my best. Not sure the hospital will have that. If not, I'll see if I can have you one sent over from one of the nearby restaurants."

"That would be cool. Thank you!"

He picked up the phone by her bed. It had a direct line to the kitchen. They didn't have any steaks available, so he got on his cell phone and ordered her a rare T-bone from Steakhouse. Done, he took his seat again.

"Thank you, Darren!"

"You're welcome, hon."

She leaned back then and closed her eyes. "I'm just going to rest my eyes for a few minutes. They feel really dry."

"Good. You do that." He leaned his head back against the wall and closed his eyes too. He dreaded what tomorrow would bring, but at least he was thankful she was alive. Even more so, he was thankful that he was alive.

Doctor Jamison was exhausted. He'd been about ready to finish his shift when Nancy had flat lined. It had happened so fast. Then for her to actually come back! It was almost unbelievable. He was still having trouble assimilating all the weird things that were happening lately. There just weren't any sensible, scientific explanations for them.

At his locker, he pulled out his coat and a small package. He'd found a book he wanted to read available on Amazon and had it delivered to the hospital. It had arrived for him that morning, but he hadn't had a chance to look at it yet. He tossed his white coat into the linen bin and shrugged into his raincoat, and then stopped long enough to unwrap the book, tossing the packaging into the wastepaper basket in the corner. *All You Ever Wanted to Know about Vampires* was written in blood-red ink across the otherwise black cover. He slipped the book into his briefcase and headed for the elevator. He planned on doing some reading after he had dinner with his wife and twin, ten-year-old sons.

Chapter Ten:

Mona squeezed into Gavril's side, clutching his arm affectionately as she gazed upon the ornate casket in the yellow lighting of the storage unit where he had placed it after his arrival to the states. "It's beautiful! The dark mahogany and the circle of red rubies on the top, with the gold leaves around the lid edges are exquisite. I don't believe I've ever seen such a luxurious casket." She tilted her face up, beholding him with great admiration.

"You don't expect me to spend my daylight hours in transit in just any old casket, do you?"

Smiling amiably, she replied, "I suppose not." She thought about it a minute. "So, this is how you came to the states? In this casket?"

Her questions did not seem to bother him, only to amuse him. "It is the way I always travel when going by sea or air. Can't risk being caught out in the daylight. We don't last long in direct sunlight, as you already know." He snapped his finger. "Poof! We light up just like a matchstick."

"And there's room for the both of us in there?"

"Yes, my love." He hunkered over and opened the casket for her to see.

The white lining was almost as impressive as the outside. "Is that silk?" she asked, touching her fingers to the smooth sides and the pillow case that held a large pillow, soft as any she'd ever felt.

"The finest silk one can buy."

"The casket is spacious."

"I assure you, my love. We will be more than comfortable." He smiled with self-satisfaction. "Plus, see these pockets here?" he said, inserting his fingertips into one of the ruffled edged pockets that trimmed the sides. "I am going to fill these with units of blood for us to feed on while we travel. I'm afraid it will be a few days before we set ashore again."

"You've thought of everything."

"I should. Not exactly new to all of this. What's more, I want my future bride to be as comfy as possible." He turned then and went over to a large cooler he had sitting a few feet from the casket. He lifted off the lid. The cooler was filled with units of blood. He began taking them out and inserting them neatly in the pockets around the casket. She zipped over and helped him. They were done in less than a minute. He put the lid back on the cooler and set it aside. "Not going to worry about this. We won't need it any further." He turned his head upwards. "I hear the truck coming for the casket now." He bowed slightly and indicated for her to climb in the casket first. She did. Soon as she was in, he slipped in beside her and closed the lid.

"It's really dark," she whispered.

"I know, my sweet. But you will get used to it. At least we have one another. This trip will be much more pleasant for me, now that I have my mate with me."

The voices of two men were heard outside, and the casket was moved and bumped around slightly as they hoisted it up on a dolly and rolled it up a plank and set inside the truck.

"Do not worry," he whispered in her ear. "Just think how much time we have to make love while we travel."

"Yes…" she replied, musing over the idea happily.

He kissed her then, and they ever so quietly held one another in embrace while they were carted off to the freighter. Once loaded, and no humans could be heard moving around close, they shared a couple of units of blood, and then passed the time making love as the boat pulled away from shore.

As promised, Darren spent the night at the hospital with Nancy. It was a sleepless night though, and it wasn't only due to what he knew he must do first thing, call his dad, it was also because Nancy had really gotten on his nerves. She hadn't seemed tired at all, talked incessantly through the night. Kept complaining about being thirsty, no matter how many times she was given water or juice. At one point, she had asked if she could get some raw liver, but was quickly informed that none was available. Darren and the little Hispanic nurse that was there at the time both shared questionable glances over that one.

When Nancy wasn't complaining about being thirsty, she was joking and laughing as though nothing had ever happened. Her mood swings were driving him nuts. He was sure the nurses thought it all a bit unusual, but if they did, they didn't address it. Just said they were happy to see her doing so well.

Darren wasn't so sure. There was something in her eyes, too. Didn't look right, but the look was vaguely familiar. He didn't want to address it, though. Didn't want to figure out what it was. He was too tired of it all. Too drained. In fact, jail was beginning to look inviting.

He was glad when seven a.m. came around, and he could call his dad. He waited until they brought Nancy's morning tray and then excused himself, saying he needed to call his dad and stepped out into the hall, but he could see Nancy from where he stood.

A pudgy redheaded nurse sat the tray on Nancy's bed. "Ham and eggs this morning, young lady."

"Good! I'm starving," she replied. "But are you sure there's no raw liver in the kitchen?"

The nurse looked at Darren out in the hall and shrugged. He shrugged back, and indicated, swirling his finger around at his temple, that Nancy was a little nuts.

She suppressed a smile and went to straightening the room.

Darren turned his back to the room just as Michael answered his phone. "Dad, I know you're busy," he said, voice heavy. "But this is very important. Can you drop by the hospital on the way to the office?"

Michael briskly stated that he would and hung up.

Darren turned back around just in time to hear the nurse ask Mona why she had it so dark in the room.

"I don't know. My eyes kind of hurt... Dry."

"Well a little sunshine never hurt anyone."

"Sure," Nancy replied, looking down at her tray of ham, eggs and toast.

The nurse went up to the window and yanked on the cord, pulling the drapes wide open. "There! Isn't that—?" She didn't get to finish.

Nancy screamed as she burst into flames.

Spinning around, the nurse's hands flew to her face. *"Oh my God!"*

Darren was still speechless and sitting out in the hall when his father arrived.

"What's going on, Darren?"

Darren didn't answer. He simply pointed to the room filled with hospital staff, police officers, and a bed covered with ashes that had once been Nancy.

The end

About the author:

Elaine Waldron is the author of "Powers", her first vampire series, along with other vampire, paranormal and murder-mystery thrillers. She began her career as a novelist with Publish America. Aside from her novels, she has had numerous short stories published in various magazines and anthologies, such as Amazing Journeys and Trail of Indiscretion, winning best story based on cover art for issue #4. She was a newspaper journalist earlier on in her career, but shortly after leaving the newspaper, she began selling her short stories.

An outdoor enthusiast, she enjoys the woods, nature in general, and loves to hear birds sing. She works with a cup of coffee or a cold Coke at her side; delights in children, and has four of her own.

Other Books by Elaine Waldron:
Powers Series – Transition, Blood of Vampira, and Blood of Angels, with Hope (book   five) in the works.
My Vampire Hero
Deep Shadows
The Vampires of Petersville, Maine
Several murder mysteries and a couple of science fiction novels.

www.ingramcontent.com/pod-product-compliance
Lightning Source LLC
Chambersburg PA
CBHW071233130626
46556CB00003B/992